THE HAUNTING

Other books by Jean Marie Rusin
Ghosts
Eye OF Tiger Roar
Mysterious Nights, Séance Ghostly Haunting
Willow Lakes Haunting
Long Silky Blonde Girl
Broken bridge Lies the body of water
Thin ice zombies in LA Nowhere to run or hide
Thin ice zombies in LA Nowhere to run or hide Returns
Thin ice zombies in LA Nowhere to run or hide Battle
A Polish story with a magical Christmas tree
Memories of love
Spooky
Night of terror
Poison Pen Pal

JEAN MARIE RUSIN

EDITED BY N. Y. T. B. S.

authorHOUSE®

AuthorHouse™ LLC
1663 Liberty Drive
Bloomington, IN 47403
www.authorhouse.com
Phone: 1-800-839-8640

Published by AuthorHouse   02/06/2014

ISBN: 978-1-4918-6292-6 (sc)
ISBN: 978-1-4918-6293-3 (e)

CONTENTS

INTRODUCTION

Our home was a typical tri-level from the '70s. I lay at the bottom in the caboose, the small room in the basement on the basement on the backside with a convenient set of double doors that frequently allowed us boys to escape late in the night.

When the music played, I was in guitar heaven, loving the solitude, taking in the Pizza.

My eyes adjusted to the darkness that filled the room and everything took on a blue-Purple sheen.

Looking straight ahead, daydreaming, usual, something caught my attention.

The adjacent room had been vacant and blue. No one had entered or exited for the half hour or more that I had been down there—until the shadow moved.

I lifted my eyes to see a form step out of the darkness. A full-bodied figure silently walked in front me, looking forward then abruptly turned to the left, staring down at me. There were no eyes, no face, No teeth glimmering in the moonlight. The figure was midnight and quiet as the morning.

It took another step and its body faded into eternity.

Old house, broken crack pipes and scorched spoons and up lighters.

She had convinced herself what she had seen through the crack in her bedroom.

Because reality trumped imagination every time, she thought.

That's how things worked, wasn't it?

She had recognized the thing when she saw it. It had appeared as something that couldn't be here, but she didn't care.

She looked away to the window and the ghost beyond.

Once the ghost came, she had tripped over steps and landed on floor.

She was Afraid what happened next.

Base on true events.

CHAPTER 1

Ghost House

We picked the nicest house on The Block. IT's medium, but for us, it was just right.

If you open the front door, you walk right into the living room eight by ten feet large. Walk further in and you'll be standing in the dining room.

Now you have a choice to make—left turn to the tiny bathrooms and three bedrooms; going straight will get you into the kitchen. There's a door near the back left of the kitchen leading into the basement and the backyard. Water fills the basement when the rains, but it's rather big; besides the water coming in, it's rather big; beside the water coming in, its only flaw is the height of the ceiling—one has a duck occasionally if stands the height of five-foot ten. The crowing jewel, however, of the entire house, is its attic.

Though tiny, in perfect conformity with the rest of the place, it is carpets and stretches back by the way of tall hallway to the door through which lies a wide, inhabitable space above the living room and bedrooms. The stairs leading to it accessed from the bedroom we used a den room, furthest from the back door.

A yellow porch juts forward into a quiet street, and sitting thereupon on a quaint fall afternoon, one spies the green of the park across the street. A set of swings seldom move in the soft wind, and beyond them, the playground leads by the fence into wide often— trimmed, soccer field, discovering a one-tenth of a mile's depth of impenetrable woods. Follow their edge through, and you would pass track on tenth of mile long in circumference, and rounded oblong course with a heart of mown grass. The town quiet, ordinary suburb; it is noisy with children at the height of day, but silent as death at night. When you walk across the street to the swings, then through the fence into the soccer field, you are guided by yellow streetlights, which flicker a constant, artificial greeting. Sewage lines run beneath the playground, and the light is often accompanied by their wandering smell. Planes roar overhead, and most everything is peaceful;

To this place, I wish never to returns.

I was tired, but Kathy needed a walk.

One per day is no good, and so the onset of guilt drove me to get the dog and put the leash on the dog.

Kathy took the dog for the walk and about one hour.

The street was quiet as usual, the neighbors' house light on, with no one in the playground. I crossed to the other side, away from the glow of our porch light, into and under the ambiance of the artificial yellow street posts.

Already Kathy crossed her expendable leash around her dog legs, running away to investigate the night habits of a cat. I reeled her on in, secured the leash's locked so that she'd stay within several feet, and strode on through the fence and into the soccer field. We wandered aimlessly across the wide expanse—she following invisible trails in the grass, and I looking up placidly at the barely visible stars. Planes roared, very low to the ground, powering on toward their destination in Windsor, Connecticut, just five miles to the north. From my left came the only other noise of the night, a chorus of crickets, their harmony emanating from the edge of the dark customary route around the track. Katy taught me to be more present, as she always was in her life.

I noticed something confusing: customary was my inclination to poke my finger into the palm of my hand when such moments of puzzlement occurred, for that was a good test to see if I dreamt, or really was awake. My finger did go through my palm of hand I believed i saw a vision in front of the window of our bedroom.

Within the glowing square a human had moved; someone was inside our home.

'A stranger is my house. I live diamond road on ruby Avenue.

I am in my bedroom, and I saw someone standing in my room.

Yes I am in my house—I saw in the living room.

I hear rumble sounds and footstep coming closer to me, and my husband Kevin is not here. Then the increased and blinding strobe lights whipped around my home.

I haven't found anything.

I felt calmed, and proceeded to stayed in the house.

Kathy bounded in, aware of the strange occurrence.

As I tried to go to sleep in an unfamiliar bed that night, I began to question my sanity, and the vision that had gripped me that evening. I did not doubt the authenticity of sighting had I been unsure, I would hesitated to call Kevin.

I had overacted instantly, been filled with dread and excitement immediately.

Before I fell asleep, I relived the night's events at least two more times.

Time passed and the strange sight was soon forgotten.

I had seen it, and I guessing at his ghost invading my house.

He'd been a little more than half the height of window.

I soon fell upon a dreadful idea that persisted until one night I bought it up to him bed:

If someone came into the house, which we have accepted did actually happen, and I saw the shadow.

"That's ridiculous.

I fell asleep that night feeling for first time at peace with had happened.

Although I wished that the experience had been shared—that someone else had seen and could confirm what startled me that night—I felt as if Kevin was right why would someone was there.

The next morning ended my newfound serenity in record time. I poured my morning coffee, prepared to depart for shopping.

I inform him there was something urgent he needed to see, she put aside her table and will show its Kevin later.

I saw a horrifying in my kitchen when I was leaving the house.

No one really seemed to notice that something was wrong with me all throughout the day. I can't stop worrying.

A wave of relief coursed through me. I would have access to every ghost story, and they would be able to subdue my reformed fear.

Would tell me my fears were groundless, as I hoped.

A ghost of the man was present, dressed in a suit; ghost I instantly surprised.

I was not able to speak, at that moment.

Ghost was staring at me and I was just frozen and I couldn't move.

Kathy's lost her sense of smell that day.

Then the ghost guided Kathy to the old musty closet its morbid contents.

Within several dark shadow was showing me the dead body that was cut up into pieces, and then the shadow was gone.

I called the police, and two squad cars arrives the front of my house.

"Yes, I wanted to know about the murder in your house?

I have been dispatched to your house for questioning. Kathy is speaking to them now. I will be able to be in my house after the crime scene.

For an hour the police stayed with us. They asked to recreate the night of the crime, and Kathy said a ghost show me this body.

"At that time, we can only guess the criminal was looking at your place to store the body that night."

"Do you have any idea who the victim is yet?"

"We have an early lead, but it's not confirmed, that at that time Star was communicating with the ghost in this house.

She heard shuffling of boots against the wall and the dog started to bark and the back door was open, it was like a whoosh just a chill in the air.

About a minute later the door closed and the dog was staring at the door, and I saw the shadow coming close to me.

One night I was left alone and I thought that I was going to get attacked.

A half hour—hour passed and darkness came through me and it felt, more occurs and events when I am home alone.

That night I woke up at two in the morning. A noise sounded, like metal hitting the wall.

"Did you hear that?"

"Yes I did.

The sound we'd heard, that had taken us for second time from our peaceful sleep, and once again, we heard it.

The location was the attic without question, in the wide section, portion directly over our beds. IT wasn't quiet metal on concrete—it was the grating of a hinge, used hinge, the crack of the rusted door that hadn't been used in years.

Voices and the whisper at night, and sometime the pots and pans make noise and Judy said no I don't, and don't you feel the chill in the air, and have cold breathe, and Judy once again said no I don't hears that you are lying.

Then Kathy came home and said what is the commotion going on here and Kevin said you would not understand, try me, okay, do you ever feel that you are not alone? No, what going on here and Judy said to her daughter some kind of occurs happen and they cannot be explains. Like what mom, Kevin said like footsteps and like voice and sound and what else and then Kathy said well he must be taking drugs, why do you says that?

Well this house is nice and no one is here, and not a ghost and Kevin said to Kathy, you are a skeptic, I might be and I don't believe in ghosts.

So that is your opinion and that all I will says, and Kathy when up to her room and said started to laughed and Judy said why are you laughing at your brother? She said he flip out of his senses, and stop crucial him so much.

Then she slams the door and put her CD and music was on and listens to the music and then she said stop knocking at the door and she got up and there was no one there, and she then when down and said Kevin why did knock at my door? I didn't go upstairs and I was with mom, is that true, mom and she shook her head. She's was terrify for her life and our lives.

CHAPTER 2

Seeing Ghosts

One late night Judy when to the basement to put the do the laundry and she just put on the light and then it started to flicker and then suddenly the light when off, and Judy felt a chill in the air and felt a cold air and someone just touch her shoulder and then the light when back on and Judy decided to go back upstairs and walk upstairs and decide not do wash that night, went she was walking up the stairs, she saw a partial apparition, on the wall of the stair.

But now Judy felt more cold chill in the air and seem like it was going to follow her and so she hurried up and shut the door quickly and lock it and when to her bedroom and then she decided to take a shower and so she when into the bathroom and when toward the shower and put on the water and open the curtain and then she undress her jean and pull over blouse, and threw it on the floor and remove her pink pantie and when into the shower and close the curtain, and then took the soap and wash over all her body and it was foaming and wet toward her skin and then she was about to rinse off the soaking soap off her body and then suddenly something grab her into the shower curtain and she was not able to get loose and she was calling out for help and then about ten minute later, Kevin ran in and took curtain and rip it open and Judy fell to the floor and Kevin wrap his mom with a blue beach towel and said mom are you okay? At first she was quiet and didn't say anything at all, and she looks into her eyes and she was a fear looks and was terrify, what just happened to her.

But she didn't want to talk about it and so Kevin left her alone and when back to his room and Kathy came out and said what just happen to mom?

I don't know but it was not human and it was a ghost that attack mom. I don't understand but I need to called dad and tell him what happen to mom.

You know that dad doesn't believe in the paranormal and he will be angry if you called him at work, but someone has to be with mom and Kathy said I will stayed with mom, are you sure? Yes and we both will be fine.

About two hour later, Kevin was just sitting in his room and so he heard a sound that was coming from the attic and so he was going to check it out but he didn't tell anyone what he was going to do.

Meanwhile Judy and Kathy talked about how she convince James to buy this old house and Judy said the first time that I saw it and I fell in love with it.

I will tell you tell you why I fell in this old house and I think I might be repeating myself and so the history and the wood work and I just wanted it and it was like a possession to have it and but your dad said it were be probably expensive, but it was not and we got it for a good prices, but mom I think that we have residence living here all ready, what do you mean that we have residence, I mean that we have ghosts here. No that is nonsense, you might hear a creaking sound, and it is an old house and that is nothing wrong, about the shadows, just when it is dark and it is only when car come by and Judy said, it is only your imagination, no it is not, now you sound like dad. I do not want to argue with you and so I am going to bed and Judy just dismissed it and but she just forgot what happen to her in the shower, so Judy when to bed and turned off all the lights in the house and about one hour later she heard thumping and then heavy footstep coming toward her and she thought it was her son Kevin and she got up and when to her door and open it and it was no one there!!

Judy looks around and when back to her bed and then she felt a chill in the air and felt that someone was with her and now Judy was threaten and didn't called out for anyone but sat on the bed and started to pray to god and somehow she felt asleep and woke up the next morning and all her clothes were shatter on the floor and then James came in and said what are you doing what your clothes and at the moment Judy, was speechless and didn't says anything at all. James came closer to Judy and kissed her lips and hold her tight and gave her a hug and said, I am very exhaust and so I need to go bed and she said, I will join you and he said of course and then they fell asleep, and they woke up and they heard a scream and it was Kathy and they both got up and Kevin was the first got to Kathy room and Kevin asked what wrong and she said I had a nightmare and it was gruesome and I don't want to talk about it and then Judy and James came in and said what wrong honey, and she answer, I had a terrible dream and we would all dead, and Judy said, it was just an nightmare, and go back to sleep and then they all when back to their room and they slept and about 315 am, the clock started to click loud and Judy got up from the bed and went downstairs and then she saw an entity, staring right at Judy and it was almost a whole figure, and Judy just ran back upstairs and didn't says anything and just got close to James and hold him tight.

Next morning Kevin was the first one downstairs and he walks to the kitchen and the fridge was open and the foods was threw out on the floor and milk was spill on the floor and then Judy got up after him and she said, Kevin what have you done? I have didn't do this and Judy said don't denied it,

CHAPTER 3

Sleepwalking

Kevin said mom I didn't do this and who did? I don't know mom and so she just said clean it up and don t let your dad to sees this, he will be angry and he will yelled, and so Kevin started to clean the mess and he took the mop from the closet and then something just knock him off his feet and Judy ran into the kitchen said what happen and he said I don't know, but he got up and clean up the mess and then Kathy came down and she was like in a daze and Judy was talking to her and but she didn't answer and James said that Kathy is sleep walking and so we cannot wake her up but I will take her back to her bedroom and when they got to her room it was so cold and chill in the air and then he saw her window was open, but first her walk her to her bed and she lay down and slept and then he tried to close the window and then it were not shut down.

Then he tried one more time and then it close and then Kathy woke up and said dad what are you doing in my room and then he asked why do have your window open, and she said I didn't open it and he said probably when your sleep walking, dad I don't sleepwalking and I didn't do that for an long time and so what are saying dad, and then Kathy saw a shadow and was afraid to tell her dad and James said did you see something and she nodded her head and said yes I did, and he said, I don't believe in GHOST, and he said it is your imagination and that all.

No this house is haunted and you never listen what I am saying and now you are saying that you are a physic, no but I do see them and you can asked mom she had an experience in the shower, and once again it just in your mind,

Dad your such a skeptic and you don't believe us and your never home to see what going around in this house and then Judy step into the room and said stop the nonsense and your dad work too long to listen to this stuff that might not be going on and Kevin came in with a camcorder and said I will tape and prove it for once for all, fine.

Kevin when back to his room and Judy and James, left and Kathy was left alone and she felt a sleep once again and about half hour later Kathy was walking downstairs and when into the kitchen and open the fridge and the camcorder was running and then she grab the milk and drank it from the container and then took some eggs and threw them on the floor and then sat at the table and was like talking with someone and then she walk upstairs and when back to bed and slept and then next morning Kevin looks at the tape and said, looks mom and dad look what Kathy is doing, and James and Judy were very upset about Kathy at this point.

Then the low humming noise and then light footsteps coming toward Kathy bedroom and then it stops and then Kevin got up and looks around and then he went downstairs and then something just put him up in the air and he started to yelled and scream and then he was dropped to the floor and they came running down and said what happen and he said something pick me up and they said, you probably just trip and fell, once again no one didn't believe him on the third day, of move and so he got up and said looks I have a cut and bruise and Judy said you will be fine and they all when back upstairs but they didn't looks at the table that all things were blow off and on the fourth day Kevin said I will be camera in every room to catch what I am seeing sure.

Judy got up and went downstairs to the kitchen and saw the pots and pans on the floor and eggs scatter on the floor and the basement door was open and she shut it but she felt that someone was there.

Then she saw the front door open and then she shut it and Kathy came out screaming and said, I have bees in my room and I don't want to be stung, and they rush into her room and nothing, KATHY your sleepwalking is making you think that you having something in your room, Kevin said she might be delusion, stop it.

Then Kevin said, why don't we tried the Ouija board and contact someone and Judy said no, you will be inviting evil forces, but Kevin said okay mom and then he went into his bedroom and took out the board and started to asked questions and Judy walk in and she was furious with Kevin and what have you done? I didn't do anything mom and she took the Ouija board and threw it out in the trash and about five hours later it was back in the house. Judy said Kevin you bought the Ouija board back in the house and he said no mom, and why is it on your shelf in the closet and but mom I didn't bring in and then Judy took out of the closet and then when downstairs and then put her jacket and when outside and put on a charcoal grill and the fire was burning and then threw into the fire and it were not burn and then she broke it into pieces and once again the trash and then the next day it was in the kitchen table and it was whole and Judy couldn't believe her eyes.

CHAPTER 4

Ouija board

Judy didn't know what to do with the Ouija board and so she put in the garage and so she put into a wooden box and lock it and the next morning once again it was in the house and now Judy didn't know how to deal with the Ouija board.

She knew that Ouija board is an evil forces that can comes in and it was all her son fault by using the Ouija board and now she have to asked someone how to get rid of it now, then Kevin came home from school and saw the Ouija board on the kitchen table and his mom step out and when to the store and then Kathy came home and when to Kevin and said, let use the Ouija board and he said, no we will bring in evil forces in the house, do you believe in that's and Kathy started to fool around and asked, the first question was are we in danger and it pointed, yes and who will get hurt and then it started to spell her name and she said, stop pushing Kevin and he said I am not moving it.

But who is moving it and I don't, and then Judy came home and asked did use the Ouija board and Kathy was about to say yes but Kevin nodded his head and she said no, are you telling the truth, and Kathy said of course, mom.

Later that night, Kevin and Kathy went upstairs and Judy was sitting at the table and then she got touch and she looks around and no one was around at first she thought that James was home, or one of the children.

About a minute later, she heard footsteps coming toward her and she thought it was Kathy but it was a shadow, and she looks and then it was gone, and then she thought, I must be losing my mind and then the phone rang and then it was James on his ways home and then he said, do you want me to pick up a pizza and soda on the way home and Judy said, yes that were be good and then James said, so what do you want on the Pizza, and Judy said well let get pepper and onion and meatball but not extra cheese about the kid, well Kevin like Cheese and eggplant and onion and Kathy, so get a cheese pizza, and she will like it, oh one more thing, light on the cheese and extra sauce., got it.

Then suddenly the phone disconnect and the light started to flicker and the low humming noise began, and light whisper, and footsteps coming closer and then the table was moving and Judy got up and a chair almost hit her and then it pick her up and put way out in the ceiling and then it drop her on the floor and then Kathy came down and saw her mom laying on the floor and said, mom are you okay? Judy nodded her head and said I am fine.

Then object would flying around and Kathy then confess to her mom that she was fooling around with the Ouija board and Judy said HOW COULD YOU, I WARNS YOU NOT TO PLAY WITH THE OUIJA BOARD. I am sorry mom, I didn't think something like this would happen and then Judy said pick me up and then Kevin came down said what happen to mom? She got touch and drag from a ghost, no kidding, really mom, yes and then she back was bruise and cut and then she put the Ouija in the box and took it to the attic. One night James came home from work and called out Judy and said, I am going into the attic and getting the Ouija board and Judy said, no you are not, your son and daughter make enough problem with it and now we have a " dark shadow" in the house and he said, I need to tell you that we move in a haunted house and there were many death and Judy said I thought you didn't believe in ghosts, I don't, so what the harm of getting the Ouija board and asking question and calling for the one that are gone and try to reach them, so ok we can try that's are sure, said Judy to James, yes let do it tonight, so James when up to the attic and took out of that wooden box and put on the kitchen table and lit some candles and then he hold on Judy hand and said some words and then it started to work, and Judy said what are going to asked and he said, are we going to dies in this house? Judy said I don't like that question and it move and it said yes.

So asked a question and Judy said, will be fine and will my children be safe? It answered no!!!

Judy got up and left him with the Ouija board and James asked who are you?

It answer, Jon, once I have lived here and now, and your family will live here, has residence and the house will not let you go and it has forces and then Jon was gone!!!

James got up from the kitchen table and went to get a drink and James, got himself a scotch and water and sat back down and then Judy said are coming to bed and he said I am staying up for a little while and I put the Ouija board back into the attic and Judy said you don't have do it tonight and then James pull out the ladder to the attic and now he was hearing a low humming sound and he then he heard footstep coming toward him and he thought it was Judy and then a second later, James fell down and lay on the floor until morning and Judy found him and he was laying there and she tried to wake him.

CHAPTER 5

Attack by ghost

Judy when to wake him but he didn't wake up and then she saw blood on the floor and then she shook him and then he open his eyes and said what happen to me? I don't know and then a few minutes, Judy and James heard some thumping and humming sound and then a few footsteps coming toward them.

About one hour later, Kathy and Kevin got up and said what happened and Judy said, well your dad and I use the Ouija board and so it just hurt dad and now he must have to go to the hospital and James said I am not going and I have go to work and when he was getting up and saws the ghosts and he said don't you sees them? Judy said no I don't and Kevin said they are here.

They are standing right next to you and they wants us and you are not making any sense right now, the bump on the head you are delusion and so I think that I will take you to the hospital and he got up and said I am going to take a shower and go to work and Judy said no you are not. Yours going stop me, yes I am stop you and he said I need to go and I will have a new client with a lot of money for the firm and Kevin said I have a premonition and you should listen to mom, and now I am going, and so went upstairs and when into the shower and got dress and got his computer and briefcase and keys and walk down the stairs and went to kiss Judy and said bye to his children and close the door behind him and when to the car and when inside and started up and drove away and

15

Judy said, well Kevin and Kathy get ready for school and Kevin said I am worry about dad and Judy said me too!!

Kevin and Kathy left for school and Judy was left alone and now she when to the laundry room and do the wash and then she was not alone and then she said Kevin are you home and but she felt a chill on the air and then something touch her and she was frighten at that point and then the phone rang and it was James and said, well I will be going to the west coast tonight with Henry and she said that is your boss and he said yes and so I will be back next week and so will you and the children will be fine and she said sure we will be.

James said, something wrong and she said no, nothing wrong and then he said, I love you and she said I love you too, and then she heard a growling sound and she didn't know where it came from and low humming noises and whispers and then it touch her again and she stood there and couldn't move at that moment and Kevin came home from school and called out mom are you okay and nothing and so he saw the basement door open and then he went down and saw his mom standing in fears, and her eyes were strange and he went to her and gave her a hug and she said I am glad that you are home.

Kevin tried to ask what was wrong and Judy refuse to says, but she said your dad will be out town for five days, on business, Judy said we are not safe, I think it attack your dad and it will attack us too, and Kevin said we cannot leave and it will follow us, how do you know that's? I just know that.

Kevin said we need to warns dad not to take that plane trip to LA and Judy said why not and it will crash and Judy said, well I called dad and tell him not to go on the plane and Kevin said hurried and Judy said his cell is going to voice mail box and so I cannot reach him, why don't just drive up to the airport and Judy said that is a good idea and I will go alone and Kevin said I am coming along too, and Kathy said I am coming too.

No, you both go to school and so I will catch your dad and I will not be late, so Kathy and Kevin got ready for school and waited for the school bus and Judy got her keys and when to the car and got inside and started up the engine and drove off and Kathy said I am skipping school today and Kevin said that is a good idea and Mom will not know that we did.

About half hour later, when Judy drove to the airport and when she got there and he was not there and then she page him, but they couldn't locate him and then Judy waited in the terminal and then she saw him walking with his boss and she ran up and said you cannot go and I need you home., and his boss looks strangely at her and James took on the side and said what are you doing and she said that Kevin had a premonition and so he is danger and he said I am going and I sees you in a week and then his boss said what wrong with your wife and he said she is very overprotection and so he laughed and wave to Judy and meanwhile at home Kevin once again took out the Ouija board and Kathy said let hold hands and asked questions and so Kathy asked is my family in danger and it move to yes and then Kevin asked should we leave and it move yes and Kathy and Kevin said we should leave and called mom from a hotel and we can stayed there for three days and Kathy said mom will not allow it and so sit down and let continue asking question and the next question is who will get killed and it said James, oh my god dad will get killed and Kevin said hope that mom will stop him and about one hour later Judy drove home and the lights were on and she came in and Kevin said, where dad and she said left.

CHAPTER 6

Premonition

Kevin said mom I have a really, really bad feeling about dad going to LA, and something will happen to him and she said how do you know, I just have gut feeling and I cannot explains it and then she asked and said, I sees the Ouija board on the table and it more that you asked and not a premonition and yes and I did warns you not to play with it and I was not home and you too, are in trouble and I will deal with you later and she went into the kitchen and make coffee and then she said that we are going to have pizza, and I will make the decision what kind and they will delivery and so that fine mom and so she order a large New York Style and cheese and then one onion and pepper and thin crust and then she gave the address and it will take about half hour and Kevin said I will be in my room doing my homework and she said fine and then Kathy kept her mom company and then the doorbell rang and Judy went to the door and thought it was the pizza guy but it was a neighbor and so they said welcome to the neighborhood and so Judy said thank you and bought in the cake and then went back and she was still standing and Judy said come in and said no I am not stepping a foot in that house and Judy said why not and then she said I got to go now and left in a hurried and now seem like a mist over the house and a bit of heavier in the air and Judy was like out of breathe and Kathy said mom are you all right and she nodded her head and said yes I am fine and then sat down Kevin said what wrong with mom and then he said they are here, and Kathy said who is here, the peoples that use to live here and you don't make any sense Kevin.

About ten minute the pizza arrive and Judy answer the door and paid the guy and he just took off and Judy said what wrong? Kevin open the box and took piece of pizza and started to eat and then Judy said I will give a some soda and they said yes we like that and then she open the fridge and saw the foods spoils and some bugs crawling and Judy close it fast and Kevin said what wrong mom? She said look in the fridge and he's did everything was okay and then she said, it fine and then pour the soda into the glasses and they sat down and ate and later Kevin said I forget to shut the TV in my room and so he got up and now it was an eerie sound and a lot thumping and the lights were flicker and the door just open, and Judy looks and the temperature drop and someone was with them. One day things started to happen more like objects flying off the shelves and landing on the floor and James still doesn't believe what they are saying but Kevin said, we need to warns dad on his trip, their an bad accident and someone will die and Judy said not dad and Kevin couldn't answer and Judy said, no, he will be fine, said Kevin and Judy said are you sure about that, and you are not lying to me? But Kevin didn't says anything and just got up and left the room and said, we are not alone here, I believe that we have ghosts in the house and some are good and some are evil, and some are partial body and they want to control us and Judy said how do you know and Kevin said one is standing right next to you and Kathy came down screaming and Judy said what wrong I just saw a little boy in the hallways, and he was with dark eyes and staring at me, and I thought he were grab me . . . let me go, Kevin pull his mom but then it pulling her back, then an eerie and then Kevin, said don't take her and the thumping started, then the footsteps would coming closer and closer, and then a breeze and a cold breathe, Kevin said they are here, one of them is standing right next to you mom . . .

Then a whisper calling my name and then the light flickers and the doors started to open and close and I told you that it were happen and I don't want to be trap in the house and mom yours listening to us and I think that the premonition is in the house and dad is not in danger, but we are, and what are you saying?

We should have left with dad and now, it is getting worst in the house and the " dark shadows are the evil one and Kathy said listen to him and then they heard a stomp and then they saw mores of the ghosts in the mirrors with the old fashion clothing and the shoes, were like make out skin and the dress was like dark and with a hat on head and then it approach and the phone rang and Judy went to answered it is was a lot of statics and no one on the lines and then Kathy got push down and Kevin went to rescue her and then suddenly the knife fell out from the ceiling and now Kevin and Kathy and Judy were holding on together and now what?

Mom don't looks, I think that we have a poltergeist in the house and I think that we have more than that kinds, I am confuse, and then it came up to Kevin and he felt a burning on his skin and his mom look and it was on his stomach and she said, we need to go now and Kevin said they will follow us and that will not help the situation and it will not let us go, and Judy started to freak out and Kevin said mom, don't let them overpower you and they will interact and then it will be a nightmare, and Judy calm down and then Kathy got pull and Judy and Kevin tried to help her but it drag her into the other room and then they got there and she was not there!

CHAPTER 7

Vanished in thin air

Judy and Kevin search the house and then James called and Judy
answer and was not sure what to say at this point and Judy just kept
quiet about Kathy is missing and Kevin said why you didn't says
anything to dad and she said dad would just leave his business trip
and comes home and Kevin said don't we need him right now, we
will find Kathy and we will not have to worry dad and James heard
something in her voice and he asked her and she lies to him and said
everything is fine, and then he hung up and Kevin said, we need to
looks at every corner of the house to find Kathy and it we don't, and
Judy said we will find her, and Kevin was a bit scare at this moment
and Judy took out the rosary and started to pray and now they were
getting worst and things were on the floor and she saw Judy sweater
on the floor and it looks like it was in blood and oh my god and is
she dead? Kevin said don't let them win and I think I know how to
contact them and she said how?

Remember the Ouija board and Judy said, no I will not allow
it bought evil we need to called a priest and Kevin said they won't
come now!!!

Mom do you have holy water and a bible and she nodded her
head and said yes I do and let pray and get your sister back.

One hour later. They were praying and then they heard Kathy
voice and saying help me, and help me and Kevin said did you hear
that mom, she is still alive and trapped between this world and the
dead.

No, we need to get her out of the light and we need to be home with us.

Then it was nothing and Kevin said we lost communicate with her and I don't hears her voice, I don't understand what going on here but we are not safe and I believe that we should leave now and Judy said no, we need to find Kathy and then we all will leave and Kevin said that is not a good idea, mom and so Judy refuse what he was saying and they just kept on looking for Kathy and she was not there and then they heard eerie and footsteps and they were coming closer and the house was getting more heavier and heavier and Judy couldn't breathe and Kevin said now we have to go now and Judy flatting saying no I am not leaving my baby daughter alone in this creepy house. Now Kevin was seeing globe flowing in the dark and said, do you sees them and she said yes I do and that will not stop me and then Kevin went to the front door and tried to open it but it was shut tight and Judy said what wrong and he said we have a slight problem and then a moment later, Judy felt someone was staring at her and then felt her with a chill and cold breathe and Kevin said, I will be right back and I will document this and we will have proof to shown and Judy said that your dad not going to believe and then the low humming noises began and then Kevin said did you sees that lady in black and she said no, then he got knock down and then Judy got slapped on her face and then it pick her up and up to the ceiling and then drop her five feet and she fell on her stomach and was in pain and then Kevin went to helped his mom and then he saw the shadowy figure and then it came closer to Kevin and then punch him in the stomach and then he fell and Judy ran to him but then it threw her up and then down and then drag her way and Kevin said started to screams and said bring my mom back and sister and a swooshing sound and she was gone and then he looks around then the house got pitch black and the lights were out and he use his camera and just died.

Then he search for a battery and then he got hit on the face and got scratches on his stomach and back and then it push him down and the house shook and then he just was still in the living room and about five minute later, it just pick him up and drag him away and he was screaming and yelling and said leave me alone and all the doors and windows were wide open and he was gone and the phone rang and it was James and leaving the message that he was on his ways home and so he thought to himself that they probably when out to dinner and a movie and on the ways home he stop to get red roses and pizza and then he called again and no one didn't answer and it was static and a weird sound and that he never heard and so he was coming up the driveway, and he saw the open door to the house and he stop and ran inside and then the doors shut and then it was dark and he was calling out " Judy and where are you and then a minute later, he was being pushed and drag and vanished in thin air and about two month later they found the remains of James in the kitchen and was cut up and but they couldn't find the rest of the family and the police record resume missing and location authority for questionnaire and so all the neighbor came out and said once again there was an tragedy in that house and so they had yellow tape around the trees and then they left and someone said there is an girl looking out of the window and now they said this house is haunted, and time when by and but they never find Judy and Kevin and Kathy bodies in the house and so, the house stood abandon for six month and a new family move.

CHAPTER 8

New Family

Josh and Star move in with the two month baby and the house was for a cheap price and Star, said to her husband, we will never leave this place like the previous owner and Josh said to Star, do you know that they find the remains of James in the kitchen and Star said, I don't want to hear about that, I will called the priest in the morning and bless this house and she put the cross on the walls and said we will be fine and the two month ago baby started to cried and Josh said I will put an recorder in every room and we will sees if we have any " paranormal activities in the house and Star said you got to be kidding me? No!

Star took the baby to the nursery and put on the monitor and then the cat follow her into the baby room and the cat was staring and Star said who are you looking at Felix, but Star ignore what was going around her and she just was just a skeptic and Josh set up the whole house with cameras and then he saw black flies flying toward him and then he tried to killed them and then they were gone and Josh called out to Star and said I am ready heat up the steak and the potatoes and Josh was grilling them on the stove and Josh started to smell some of odor that came from the basement and then a second later smoke alarm went off. Josh said I will go and check it and Star said don't go now it is dark and the basement lights are not working, and so Josh said I will take a flashlight and Star, please don't go tonight, and okay I won't and then Star when up to Josh and kissed him and then said I need to check the baby and Josh said stayed with me and then Star, about a minute later, Josh and Star would siting patio and then Josh got up put some music and they both dance under the stars and then Star stop dancing and heard the baby crying and Star just left Josh at the patio and ran upstairs to the baby and the baby was facing down and then Star pick up the baby and when to the rocker chair and then sang a song and then she heard the footsteps and then she called out and said Josh are you out there and meanwhile Josh was sitting and then heard the whisperer and got up and when inside and when into the TV room and sat on the couch and then put on TV and then Star then put the baby back into the crib and then she saw a shadow and stop and took the baby downstairs and Josh said why did you bring the baby down? Star said. I thought the baby was in danger and then Josh said put the baby down and comes close to me.

Josh our son, Lee, and well he is only two month old and Josh said tonight I felt some weird stuff, but I don't things it is not ghostly, but the only the house is only settle, but Star said Josh, I will called the priest to bless our house, I have nothing against, and that is your choice, and I know that you will feel better, but Josh you are skeptic, I could be and Josh said, and I just want to watched the show.

So be quiet and Star said well I will put Lee but to bed and so we can have some private time together, and I will be back and so she left Josh and when back to nursery and then she felt the temperature change and Star got on the up of the stairs and then she saw an Partial Apparition, and three of them standing with a spot of grey and a long hands and she was going to scream and but she just looks and about a minute, and they were gone . . .

About one hour later Star came down and Josh was fast asleep and so Star when to the remote the TV and turned it and the TV came back on and she wanted to wake up Josh but she was scared and but sat in the dark and then the lights when came on and then they shut off.

The next morning Josh got up and then saw Star sleeping on the couch and he came up to her and she was about to jump and he asked what wrong.

Nothing and then Star check the monitor and then heard Lee crying and then Josh said I will go and see the baby and then Star said I will and she when up and saw three of them in the walls, and then Star wipe her eyes and my eyes are playing tricks on me and then they were gone.

Josh said what wrong? Nothing and why are you acting like your mad at me, no I am fine and then Josh was going up and he missed one step and Star and then Star, Josh almost fell and Star ran and grab his hand and then Josh said you save me, yes I did and a minute later, Lee was crawling on the floor and Star, and Lee was at the edge and Star grab the baby.

Star felt anxiety and scare if the baby fell and Josh said it didn't happen and thanks god and then the doorbell rang and Josh said I will get it and Star said are sure? He nodded his head and then when to the door and it was a lady in a blue short dress with a pie in the box and Josh said come on in and she refuse and said, I am fine out here and so he took the pie and thanks her and she left in a hurried.

Star called out and said who was that, one of our neighbor and they bought an apple pie, oh I sees.

CHAPTER 9

Strange happening

Josh put the pie on the table and then Star came down and said, well I will make some hot tea and lemon and so he said okay!

Star took out the cup for tea and set them on the table and then she put on the tea kettle on and Josh when to see Lee and Star when to brush her teeth and then she came down said, Josh why did you move the cup from the table? He answered and said I am still with our son Lee.

Then Josh came down with Lee and the baby started to scream and cried loud and Star came in running quick and she said did hurt the baby and he said no.

Once again Lee was staring at the kitchen window and Josh said, Lee is seeing something and Star said why don't you put the baby on the high chair and Josh did and Josh step out for a moment and then he heard a boom, and then he ran into the house and the baby was on the floor and Star came running from upstairs and said what have you done to our son?

I have done nothing but he has cut and bruises on his face and we cannot take him to the hospital and they will says that we abusive him.

So, I will patch him up and he will be fine said Judy and yes and it will be fine.

No, Lee is in danger and so are we and we need to leave this house now and Josh said, I don't believe we are fine and so will the baby.

I don't like that you don't believe what I am saying about this house being haunted and that is your imagination and so your son injure so how do you explains that's and I don't but come close to me and we will pray together and so Josh and Star pray and then Lee started to cried and she said, I think that I need to change the diaper and so she left Josh alone and he fell asleep and about one hour later, he woke up suddenly and felt like someone wanted to choke him and then Star came and said what wrong?

I don't know but I just had a weird experience in the house, and I never had one then Star said now you believe me, and that why I am going to called the priest in the morning and I will place more crosses in the house, that fine with me.

Then on the monitor Star heard Lee crying and she hurried up to see what wrong with the baby and then Star said once again I see shadows peoples coming out of the wall.

Then Josh said comes to me and he hold her in his arms and said I will protection and so she was a bit calm down and relax and then the doors and windows were opening and now Star asked Josh to explains what going on now?

I cannot explains but then they both heard footsteps and humming noises and a thud sound and a bit of eerie sound, low humming sound from the kitchen and then heard like plates falling off from the cabinet and then chairs were moving and now, some whisperer and Josh said, yes I hears it and we do have some kind of activities in the house, so let pray.

Then a thumping and a more low humming noises and then the radio goes on and then it static and voices coming and a lot whisperer and hearing footsteps and slamming the doors and windows opening up and dishes flying in the kitchen and smashing and then it stop around 5 am and Josh said, I think you should called the priest to bless the house and then Star hears that Lee starting to cried and she ran upstairs and she got to the bedroom he was fast asleep and she came back down and told Josh and said I think that we move in a haunted house, and she said no kidding and I don't want to stayed here, and Josh said those ghosts are not going chase us away.

Star said they might hurt us and then what?

They won't hurt us and how do you know that's Josh and what happen to the peoples that lived here? Are they dead? I don't know.

I am really, really, scared here and I don't want to stayed, why don't you go with Lee to your mom and stayed there for a while I will, that a good idea, said Star.

The morning Star packed a bag for her and her son Lee and she asked if Josh are coming with us and he said no I will be staying and so Star said I really don't like that you will be alone in the house and he smiled and said don't worry I will be fine and are you sure said Star? Yes!

So Star and Lee were in the car and so she started the engine and then drove off from the driveway to the street and headed to her mom house but she had a bad feeling about leaving Josh alone so she got to her mom house and left Lee with her and drove back to the house and went she drove up she saw a lot of shadows in the window and one little girl stare at her and she got out of the car and came inside and she saw Josh fast asleep and then she woke him up and he said what are you back here? I was worry about you.

CHAPTER 10

Shadows Lurking

Star when next to Josh and sat next to him and then suddenly the room got cold and it was like a cold of breathe and it was freezing and Star said we do have ghosts in the house and he said how do you know that's I must be physic and you must be with the temperature dropping and we do have some kind of activities in the house and maybe we should contact like paranormal investigate and maybe they will found something, yes why not and so Josh went to the internet and said, I will called them in the morning and then the phone rang and it was Star mom said, Lee is crying, and you need to comes now and so once again Star left Josh alone in the house and she drove to her mom house and notice that Lee had cuts and bruises on him and she said mom what have you done to your grandson and she said, nothing and Star said I am taking him back home, and then Star mom said you are accusing me that I hurt my own grandson. I don't know but I am taking him home and so Star mom said fine.

She took Lee into the car and then drove off and Lee fell asleep and went they got home it was pitch black and it seems like the lights when out and she walks inside and Josh just heard something and he got up and then he saw Star and Lee at the door and he helped her out and Star put Lee in the nursery and they both when to sleep and the camera were rolling all night and things were happening. Star said that we need to called a psychic and she might help us and Josh said, not yet, but why said Star, I think that the house is old and our imagination is just going wild and Stars said about the shadows that we are seeing, I cannot explains but I am skeptic, so you are willing to risk our life and no I am not but I don't believe in ghosts, even though you got touch.

Then an ominous sound and hearing voices and whisperer and you still denied what going on here and then they heard an crackling noise coming from the upstairs and Star said, that I need to check on Lee and Josh said the baby is sleeping and why should check and Star that I need too, and left the room and Josh just sat and looks when she when upstairs and then he got up was about to eat the apple that was in the bowl and it was gross and mold and bugs were on it and he just threw it into the waste basket and when up to the bedroom and shut the door and then he just put his head on the pillow and then about five minute that cover were coming off and he said Star stop it and he looks around and she was not in the room and then he looks at the wall and he saw his face.

The face that he saw was a man with black hair and it was a bit long, but he didn't sees his face or eyes, it was like an blank page and he couldn't believe that the man approach and came to his end of the bed and about a minute later he was gone, and how Josh was frighten and scare and he couldn't sleep and then Star came into the room and said what wrong, Josh and he was pale and white and Star said you must have seen a ghost and then he said, my cameras were rolling and I will check it out tomorrow. Are you that you want to know that we have ghosts in the house and can you handle it, of course I can handle anything okay I am just asking Josh?

Josh got up and went to view the tape and then Star asked Josh and he said the tape was blank and so Star went to check on Lee and then she pick up the baby and took it into her bedroom and then she said Josh I am hearing the low humming noise from the attic and Josh said, I will check it out and she said just be careful and I will and about one hour later Josh, put into a new tape and went outside for a walk and meanwhile Star was in the house with Lee and then she heard footsteps and called out and said Josh is it you?

But no one didn't answer and then Josh walk on the ground and walk into the wood and thought he saw something and then came

Jean Marie Rusin

Jean Marie Rusin

back and when into the house and Star said were in the house, went I called you and he said I just step inside.

Josh said well your hearing sound because the house is settling and so that is all it is and Star said, about the shadows that I saw and you did.

CHAPTER 11

Shadow Peoples

I need to asked you a question what have you seen on your tapes and don't lies to me, said Star and Josh said I didn't want to tell you but I think that we do have ghosts in the house and they are harmless and they won't hurt us and how do you know that Josh, they did hurt Lee and don't you remember that time I do and why are you asking and don't looks for trouble and we are fine.

I don't want to have an incident in the house again with our son so I decided to take him to my mom and she won't hurt him, well did forget Lee had cuts and bruises and she didn't do it to him and how do you know, she loved Lee.

But something make her do it and so now yours saying that she is possession, no but she won't hurt him take my suggest and let Lee stayed with us and we can protection him and Star said, no Lee will be better far ways from here and now yours making decision for our son, I says that he stayed with us.

Fine, I thought we would have some time together and so I will called up my mom and tell her, no!!!

Then Josh said, okay take Lee to your mom and don't be too long and I will make dinner and I will have candle light and a wine and that sound romantic and so Star pack the little a bag for Lee and then they both when into the car and drove off and meanwhile Josh, went to the bedroom and decided to take a nap and so he knew it were be a while before Star would come home and he slept for a while until the smoke alarm woke him up and Star was not home yet.

Josh got up in a hurried and went to see why the smoke alarm went off and no smoke and then he decided to put on the grill and then something touch him and he looks around and he was alone and then the phone rang and it was Star and said that the car has a flat tire and would you come and get me and Josh said, sure I will. But Josh tried to leave the house to pick up Star, and the house would not let him go, so once again Star called and said are coming and I am freezing out there, then Josh said the house won't let me go and she said fight it and you will be free.

Josh step out and then when toward his car and when inside and saw one of the shadow figure in the back seat and he didn't know what to do but he just drove away and then it was gone and meanwhile Star was waiting in the wood for Josh to comes and then a dark CAR, came and she knew it was not Josh and it open the door and she saw one inside, and she ran and ran and then Josh was coming the corner and he almost hit her and then he yelled and said why were in the middle of the street and she didn't know what to says.

Josh came out the car and took her inside and check if she was okay and she had a cut on her arm and Josh said, went we get home, I will clean up your cut and you will be fine and Star was like in shock and she didn't speak all the ways home and when they got home, Josh heard the phone rang and it was his mom and she said Lee had a little accident and I took him to ER and Josh said what happen to Lee, about 10 pm, I was making hot tea and somehow Lee got burned and Josh said we will be right there!!!

Star said what happen to our baby? Well got some burned and I told not to take him there, and I said my mom is an hazard for disaster and you just could take my word but you got our son in danger and Star said maybe it was not her fault maybe something follow me and Lee to your mom house, so you are trying to protection even though Lee is in the hospital with burned?

Star said I am not going and I am staying home and he said fine, and I will bring Lee back home where he belong and she said fine, and when into her bedroom and close the door and then Josh saw the black figure walking toward the bedroom and he wanted to scream out but he just left the house and Star said Josh is it you and then the black figure came closer to her and she said please me alone and my family, and then it just vanished in thin air.

One hour later Josh came home and all the lights were off and he carry the baby in his arms and then close the door behind him and then took the baby to the nursery and place the baby in the crib and then looks outside and saw a light and so left Lee in his crib walk downstairs and then open the door and then he got cold and a chill and cold breathe, and it was a like someone was standing next to him.

Josh didn't know what to do and he just stood and then it picked him up.

CHAPTER 12

Evil Forces

When it happen that night Josh knew that he had to tell someone and had to bring someone to get rid of the " evil forces" in the house and he could explained that he was not harm and hurt by being drag, and was on the ceiling and he knew that Star had to called the priest to bless the house but Star was just dragging her feet and thought it were be fine and then Josh got into the bedroom and saw that shadow was about to be on top of his wife and so he ran up to her and woke her up and she said what wrong?

But the dark shadow was gone and so Josh said I just want to talked with you and she said I am a bit sleepy and then said tomorrow you need to called Father John and she said, to bless the house and he said yes.

Once again Star fell asleep and then Josh was awake all night long watching over Star and about 315 am the house alarm when off and Lee was crying that what Josh thought and Josh when into Lee bedroom and he was sleeping and then the closet door open and then shut and he saw more shadows and they were following him and he was scare then he decided to get something to drink and he went into the kitchen and the pot and pans were swinging back and forth and one drop on the floor and the lights flickers and then the door just came off the hinge and the ominous sound and the humming got louder and then it slam him to the floor and he was out cold.

The next morning Star came down and ran to him felt him, and he just open his eyes and said what happen and she said I found you on the floor this morning.

Then Josh said make that called now, and it is only 7 am and they are not awake yet! Went Josh said that's Lee burst out crying and the house shook.

Star ran up and left Josh on the floor and went she reach the baby room the door was closed and she tried to open but she couldn't open it.

She banged and shove and but it nudge me and tried to knock me down with my son Lee, and but I didn't let it get me and my son and I just knew I had to run and get away but the evil forces didn't want to let me go.

But then Josh somehow came to the rescue and I was safe but I was worry about Josh and I knew that I had to called the priest and bless the house before it was too late. I knew I was hesitates about doing that's but now I know that I have too.

Josh came to me and holds me tight and said we will make and we will be fine.

Then it started and it was going after us and I was terrify that it was going to killed us and I told Josh to take Lee out the house and Josh said it were only follow us, and we need to stayed and fight it with our faith and love that we have, and Josh said I didn't know that you knew about those kind of things and one more thing we need to be positive and no negativity in the house.

No more fighting and argument and that make it stronger and Star said continues and then said Lee is going to sleep with us and not alone in the nursery.

I totally agree with you and then they kiss and then Lee started to cried and Star said I need to change his diaper and so she left the room and then Josh started to see the " Dark shadow" and he was frighten and scare but he didn't move a inch.

Star came in with Lee and said what wrong? I saw it again but it didn't touch me and so I guess we will be fine tonight, and Star said I hope so.

Star said let pray and hold hands and we will be reunited and strong and no one will part us and he said I agree honey.

About half hour later they when to bed and it was silent like dead and nothing didn't happen until the clock strike at 3:15 am and then it was like thumping and heavy footsteps and it was really dark and the house was really heavier and that Josh didn't breathe and Star said are you okay?

Then the morning came and Josh when into the shower and was washing himself and then he saw " blood in the water" and he scream, and said I must have cut myself and Star ran into the bathroom and went close to the shower and check him out and then the door slams and Josh I need to see how the baby is and she said I cannot open the door and then there was a like a chill and Josh said, it is in here and it doesn't want to let us go!

Star tried to open the door and it were not move and then Lee was crying and Josh somehow push out the door and he grab the baby and chill was like freezing, and then it pick him up and threw him on the bed and Star ran in and said stop this, don't hurt my family and then it somehow got Star and drag her.

CHAPTER 13

Bless the house

Somehow Star was safe after the evil force drag her and about one hour later, Star called the parish priest to bless the house and the parish priest said I will comes tomorrow at noon and Star said fine and then the priest said hang up your crucifix and have the rosary and says pray and do you have holy water and Star said yes I do and the priest said do it now, my child. I will father, thank you so much and I cannot live like this, and my family and I know my child.

About two hours later the priest drove up the driveway and parked his car and got out and when toward the door and rang the bell and no one didn't answer the door and then the door open and then he step inside and meanwhile Lee and Star was outside in the backyard and the Priest called out and so no didn't says anything and he took out the " holy water" and sprinkle the kitchen and then he sprinkle more holy water and then he when upstairs and into the first bedroom and he was blessing the house and saying his prayed and then the door shut and he couldn't get out of the room and then black flies came toward him and then he heard a deep voice and said get out of this house and then the door open and the Priest ran out of the house and the house door close and the Priest speed out of the driveway and when toward the church and holding his bible and praying and about ten minutes Star and Lee when inside and Star thought to herself and thought when is Priest coming over and then Star called the parish and said did Father John coming to bless the house but the phone was a lot of static and she didn't hears what he was saying and then it got disconnect and Star tried again and the phone when dead.

Josh came home from work and said did you get Father John to bless the house and she said I don't Josh.

Then Josh said looks at the crucifix they are upside down and some are on the floor and then they heard a deep whisperer and she said who is that's?

Josh said something is wrong and I just feel the heavier and dark in the house and I think that we have that evil force still in the house and I don't feel safe and I think we should leave and she said it will follow us if we do go.

I am going and I am staying and we need to pray and be positive, yes I know.

I think we should called a paranormal investigate. I will looks on the internet and we will have our house back we never had it from the beginning.

What are you saying? You heard me what I said, the first day that we move in and the things happening and you said the house noises but it was not the house but the present that we have in the house and you mean the disturbance and they are not going away and we tried to have the house bless and the priest got chase way and so what do says about that and the father Josh refuse come back and now I don't what to do? Our lives are in danger and so we need to tell them to go into the light and I think some of them are evil.

Star called Father John too comes back and Star when to make the called and it rang and then father John answered and he spoke and then the phone got static and she couldn't hear what he was saying and he said Star you and Josh and Lee must leave the house now, then it suddenly hung up and Star said I couldn't understand what he was saying but he said danger, to whom I don't Josh and then things were flying left and right and then Josh said, I think blessing the house make the situation worst and she said I think that your right.

I think your right so what are we going to do about it but I don't know but we are in danger, yes I heard that over and over you told me.

Don't be so mean and rude Josh and he said I am sorry but this house is doing something to me and I cannot explain it.

Josh just walk out of the room and left Star and Lee behind and then Josh wanted to go back inside and the door were not open and he banged so hard and Star tried to turned the knob and it were nudge and Josh was screaming and yelling let me in and I am sorry and Star said I am trying but I cannot open the door.

Star just stood there and something just touched her and she felt the cold chill and said to Josh, I felt a ghost and he said let me in now.

Then Lee started to cried and then the dark mist came over and the house started with the lights flicker and the door open at that moment Josh walks in and then he just got grab and was on the ceiling and Star cried out and said let him go now!!!

About ten minutes after it pushed Star on the floor and then took Lee and he was gone and Star said let him go and then he was gone and Josh got up.

CHAPTER 14

GHOSTS

Star said where my baby? Star started too called out Lee and she only saw footprints of the ghost that taken her child Lee. Then one ghost said, leave this place and Star said I am not leaving my child here and then it whisper your all going to died here, and then Star asked Josh did you hear what the ghost said, and he said no I have not and then it tapped his shoulder and it shown him who he was and Josh said I have a bad feeling that Lee might be dead and she slapped his face and said why did you says that's?

I don't but I feel the cold air with the breath that I take and don't see it?

Sure I do and I don't want Lee to be dead and I don't want died here so we need to found Lee now and then we can leave, they won't let go us don't get it.

Then Star heard the baby crying and she said I will found him and Josh said I will go with you and she said wait for me here, fine!

Josh called out and said they wants you too and they want me too and that why they are separate us and they will get us, stop saying that Josh.

Star climb the stair and then Josh said it following you and it in back of you and she said I don't see it and then Josh got push down on his face and Star didn't see that she just continue and when into the nursery and then the door shut tight and she saw Lee in the crib for a second and then he was gone.

The light when out and then something scratched Star on her back that blood even grip on the floor and then the phone rang and it was Father John and left a message and saying you are all in danger.

But at that time Josh was laying on the floor and about a minute later he was drag and pull into the basement and Star was being cut and bruises and was bleeding and Josh was in the basement and was surrounded by 10 ghosts and they were going to killed him and then somehow Star got away and ran to Josh and said, you are not going hurt us or harm us our religion is strong and we will be positive and we will not get defeated by you.

Star walks down like ten steps and reach Josh and she pull him up and said now it is time that we get our son back and we will not let you get him and one ghost said we have him and he is one of us and she said you are lying and I don't believe you and then once again she heard Lee and she said I know where he is, and Josh said just grab him and leave the house and Star said, we are not going to leave you so you are coming with us do you hear what I am saying?

We are not alone here and they are here and who are they? "GHOSTS"

They were here from day one and they died in this house and now they want us to be residence with them and they might get us, so you need to called Father John and Star said he won't come back because of the scare of that demon, and he won't step in this house and he told me that we are in extremely danger and we need to leave now, but we cannot because we need to found Lee but that evil ghost is trapped us here, and they have our son.

But I will go through every room of the house and we will escape this nightmare and so we will be fine and how can you says that's we don't know where they took him. Do you hear that sound and it sound like an whoosh and then some thudding and thumping and thumping and then the low humming noise, and where is it coming from and I don't but I think we should keep on moving.

Then the static come on and the lights flicker and hear the footsteps coming closer and closer and then the cold air kick and the door slams with a little chill.

It is following us and it going to catch us and I am not going to let it and so, and then they hears a whisper and it was a deep voice and partial of entity coming closer and now Star couldn't breathe and Josh said are you okay? She nodded her head and said I will be fine.

I feel that we are surrounded and we will not found Lee, stop saying that's and so Star wanted to cried and but Josh hold her and said we will not dies this house and we will find our son and he will be okay.

About a minute later, Star heard Lee saying Mommy, where are you I need you and she said he is here but we need to found that room and then we will grab him from them, and they hear what we says.

Josh said I will do it alone and she said you are not leaving me behind they might harm us and it better to stick together, but we can do more it we separate and found Lee and leave.

I am not staying alone and I am going with you and once again they heard Lee but it was really vague and low and like he was dead.

CHAPTER 15

White Noise

Josh said the voices and the static they are trying to communicate with us and Star said I only want to found Lee and I don't want to talks with them.

Suddenly the TV came on and the pots and Pans rattle and drop to the floor.

Star got closer to Josh and hold his hand and said don't let me go and he said don't worry about it and I won't and then they heard that humming sound and then Josh said I don't have a good feeling about doing this but Star we are looking for our son, I do understand, but I think that something will comes out grab us and we might end up like Lee.

We can be dealing with an poltergeist and it not good and then Josh said don't you smell tobacco, and she said no I smell popcorn, I don't how many there are in the house, then Josh said you were in a hurried to buy this house and Star said now you blaming me that I loved this house and I didn't know this house was haunted, but you convince to buy it, because you wanted our son have some place to played and now we are searching for him and we cannot found and no trace of him, they took him away from us and now he is gone, stop saying that Josh.

He is alive and I feel it and how do you know, and then they saw the blood on the wall and he said, no it is not Lee blood and she said no it is not.

45

They got to the top floor and then Josh got pull and pick up and Star tried to hold on and then she saw Lee and she went inside the room and left Josh alone in the hallway and he called out Star, where are you? At first she didn't answer and she did and she said Lee is fine and I am carry him out now and he looks and she was holding a blanket but he didn't see Lee.

Josh said where is Lee? What don't you see him in my arms? No I don't, your son is in my arms, are sure and she looks and said where is he? I just had him a minute ago, then Josh said you thought you did and they are playing your mind to think that you have Josh and I will tell you the reason is that Josh was born in this house and they wanted him and they will not give him back, I don't believe you, Josh.

Then Josh said I know where Lee is and she said where? In the attic and how do know that's I just know, take my word and let go there but the poltergeist were not let them to go to the attic and Josh that we need to do an diversion and that way we will get Lee back and she said how can we do an diversion with ghosts? I don't but I am going to tried and save all of us and not one of us.

Star ran up toward the attic and Josh was the bait, and Star ran up and saw Josh on the floor, and a ball was bouncing toward him and Star grab him and ran downstairs and Josh was trapped and Star said I will help out and the house started to make more activities and it was more than they bargain for.

The voices coming through the radio and the TV coming on and every time tried to turn it off, it just turned on and Josh said this house has a ghost and Star said I told from day one and Josh thought to himself and he just remember that something tried to drag him and then Josh said because of the blessing it just got worst and we need to get someone to found out what kind of ghosts that we have in the house. So you should go on the internet and search for a paranormal investigate and get a medium to the house. I believe that we moved in a haunted house and so we have some ghosts trying to do something to us and what are saying that they wants to hurts us?

Yes and they have Lee our son and we cannot found him and so what should we do and maybe that we get some help fast and I don't know how long that Lee will be alive and where they have him, and the time is ticking and so we better get the help now.

Listens do you hear the footsteps and I think that we are not safe here and Josh said do we leave and Star said you can go but I am staying, I am not going to leave you.

Then doors creak and then they saw the shadow of a partial apparition coming toward them and then there was a whoosh sound and then a bang and the doors were closing and opening and then it just stops.

The low humming and thudding started and then footsteps came closer and closer that Josh felt the chill of the cold of his breath.

It touch me and I felt the cold and it felt that it wanted to take me somewhere and I thought that moment I were be gone.

Then he looks at his arms and it was scratches and with some blood.

CHAPTER 16

The Marked One

Looks I got marked by the ghosts, and Star said it was not a ghost but a demon that will do bad things and it is going out control and I don't know if we will make it alive so I think that you should leave and save yourself, this house will take us and we will not be seen again, what are you saying Star.

They will make you and take you from here and I don't like what you are saying Star, and but it is the truth and the marks are from the demon and now you hear what I am saying Josh.

You are saying that we should leave this house and go and we won't get hurt and Star said I am not leaving but you should go Josh, it want you badly and it might possession you and you will need to be needing a priest and you will turn into something evil and you will tried to killed me and you might success and I will be dead.

Once again the low humming sound coming from the hallways and toward them and it is thumping and thudding and you need to go now, I am leaving you behind, and do you understand what I am saying? Yes loud and clear, we need to beat the battle, and it will not be easy and we do not want it chase us from our home, so let pray and one minute later the crucifix were flying off the walls and almost hitting Josh and then she said I have a burning on my back and can you see it and he nodded his head and said yes I do.

Josh turned around for a second and the blood was dripping off the walls and he said that is a bad sign, and she said so we should just go outside and he said yes and that is an good ideas and so they tried to step outside and the door shut. They stood still and didn't move and then they felt the breeze and cold air suddenly came in and they saw the apparition standing next to them and then she turned for a moment and the dark shadow holding a child in his hands and Star scream out and said " give my baby back" and she was ran upstairs and then tried to get her baby back and then she got shove down the stairs and Josh said, why are you harming my family and we just want to be family and you are taking it away from me.

Then the TV and the Radio when on and he heard a voices and saying, you are not leaving you will be one of us and so will your wife and your child and then the lights flicker and then windows open and close and then it stops.

Josh went to see how Star was and she was still alive but weak and he said, I am calling the ambulance and they will take you to the hospital and she said.

No, I am staying and he said, no I will get you the help and she said I am getting up and I do have some cut on my head but I am fine.

Josh pick up Star and carry her to the couch and said don't move and he got a wash cloth and wash her forehead and then she lay next to him and said don't leave me I need you and we together will found Lee.

Now it was about 1: 35 am and the house started some activity and he said listen what they are saying and she said I don't hears it.

Star fall asleep and Josh was awake and he just looks around and then it was about 3:15 am and it was a whoosh and cold air and breeze and the demon push Josh off the couch and started to carry Star up to the ceiling and then the phone rang and Josh answered and it Josh mom and said, they are in my house save me, and then it disconnect and Josh said you cannot have my mom.

I will not allow it do you hear what I am saying? Then the footsteps came and pull Josh off and scratch him deeply on the back and then threw him on the floor and he lay on his face and it was bloody.

Meanwhile somehow Star was on the floor and was crawling to Josh and said you cannot die.

But Josh didn't speak and she shook his body and said listen to the words I says and then he open his eyes and looks at her, and then he just lays there still. I am glad that you alive but you don't looks that good and so I am going to take you to the emergency room and we both will be safe and about Lee, I think that he is alive and so I don't want to lose you both so, I decided to leave for a while and then we can go back to the house but I think that they will keep you overnight and so I will comes back in the morning and I will not let you go back alone, I will not be alone I will called one of old friend and so she will keep me company and so, Josh said are you going to tell her about the paranormal activities in the house, I will not say a word about that's and she will think that we are crazy so if she sees something she will tell me.

CHAPTER 17

Psychic

Star called Connie and said, do you want to comes over and you can tells me if you tells anything in the house and Connie said okay, I am game and so Star met up with and Star took her into her car in front of the hospital and she said what wrong with Josh and she answer that he was an accident and that all she said and then Connie and Star drove closer to Star house and Connie said I cannot go there and it is evil and Star said help me out Connie do your thing.

You are asking too much of me and I didn't know that you live in that haunted house that bad things happen to good peoples. Listen you need to helped me to get my son back and they have him.

I am not going to step a foot inside and I know that if I do, it going to take AWAY. BUT STAR pleaded with her and begged her to help her to save Lee.

You know that you asking me? Yes I do and went it get dangerous you just leave, take my word, I will and then they both step inside and then the doors shut tight and meanwhile at the hospital Josh had a bad feeling and he wanted to leave but he was hook up on tubes and he tried to get lose and then the nurse came in and said what are you doing? I just wanted to go home and the nurse said you cannot go tonight but maybe tomorrow and one more things she said you have an infection and where is your wife? She left and the nurse said well do you know where she is?

Yes she is home and you will be able to reach her, and then the nurse left and it got a bit cold in the room and Josh saw the shadow standing next to him and then it was gone.

Meanwhile at the house Connie said, stayed close and you must be positive and they are all standing near the stairwell; and Star said do you see Lee, no so far I so did not see him. But I feel a present and it is touching my arms and I feel a burning on my skin, and then Connie looks at her arm and said something scratching, and then Connie said that she hears whisperer and they are calling her name and Star said, don't listen to them, they will harm you and Connie said I need to speak to them to found your son Lee, otherwise he will be lost forever.

Connie's just leave Star alone near the steps and follow the humming sound and the thudding and thumping to the top of the stairs and then suddenly stops.

Then Connie started screaming and yelling and Star run up and said what wrong and Connie said you need to leave the house immediately and do you understand what I am saying to you, Star, you are in danger and you need to go now, I am not leaving my son behind and I am, not leaving you neither.

I will found him and you need to leave now, and Star was a bit stubborn but she left but the evil forces didn't want to let her go but she did go out of the house.

Star stood outside of house and wait and wait and then she heard Connie saying leave the property now, they are outside and they will pull you back inside and so you need to get into the car and drive far away from here and don't listens to them they are lying to you and they want you back.

Star was about to walk to the car and but she heard Lee crying and it make her turned around and almost step inside and at that point Connie called out I have your son, so get into the car and started it up and Connie ran out of the house with Lee and got inside the car and they drove off and didn't looks back.

But then they drove for a mile, Star said, you just didn't bring Lee and you brought someone else too, and Connie said probably follow me out and just got into the car at the same time, but we cannot go back to the house and about a mile from here he will disappear, how do you know that's?

I just know and that all I will says and will Lee remember what happen to him and Connie said no, too young and he will forget and promise that you and your family will not go back, and Star said we need to get our stuff but Lee will be with Josh mom went we pack and Connie said that is a good idea and then two miles later it was gone and Star and Connie was relief and Connie you and Lee can stayed at my home tonight and Star said I will be going to Josh mom house tonight and that was end of discussion and then about half hour they drop Connie at her home and then they left and Lee started to cried and he was not himself.

Something was not right with Lee and then Star stops and sat in the car for a while and then she heard a whisper and said come home I need you now.

The voice was Josh and so she got out of the car and called the hospital and she ASKED HOW Josh? The nurse said fast asleep.

Once again, it was Josh and she couldn't stop hearing his voice so she drove to his mom place and brought Lee inside and said that she had to do an era.

CHAPTER 18

Voices of dead

That night Star started to hears voices of the dead and to took her to the house that the psychic warns her not to go back, so she drove up to the driveway and parked the car and headed to the front door of the house and her cell rang and it was Connie and she said don't go inside, just get back into your car now.

Then the phone got disconnected and Star open the door of the house and it drag INSIDE, AND NOW SHE WAS TRAPPED.

Now Star didn't know what to do, they were not let her go and no one to help her.

Connie had a visions someone in trouble and she knew that she had to go back to the house and she knew that Star was in trouble and now they prevent Connie to go there and the way Connie had to go on many detours to reach the house and when Connie got there, it were not let her in.

Connie was banging the door and said let me in Star, but Star was not there and then the door open and Connie step inside and the door shut close.

Meanwhile at the hospital Josh got up and got unhook and got dress and snuck out and tag a cab and told the cab drive to take him home on Lake drive, and then the cab stop and said I am not going further and you are on your own and then he just speed out and Josh walk the mile to his head.

When Josh got near the house he saw shadows there the windows and then tried to open the door and it didn't open.

Connie standing and looks around and then she looks out and wave to him to go away now, but Josh didn't understand what she was saying and then he somehow unlock the door and came in and then he saw Connie said where is my wife? She nodded her head and then he came closer to Connie and said we need to found Star and leave this place and be with your son and I will bring Star back to you and if you don't this place will devour you and me and Star and no one will know what happen to us, so just leave Josh and Josh said will you be okay, Connie? Yes you must go now and so Josh goes to the door and tried to walks out and something pull him back inside and Connie said that is an bad sign and so we need to fight it, and Josh said how can we fight it when we don't sees it? It is more difficult but you need to do it, for Lee and Star.

I feel the house is getting darker and heavier and I don't like it, so when we get to the door, you walk out and don't looks back do hear what I am saying too you? Yes I do and I will be with my son and you will save my wife from these forces, yes I will.

About ten minutes later the door open up and Josh walk out and Connie said just go and this time he just close the door and walks to his car and got inside and drove away with a blink of the eye.

Meanwhile Connie was calling out Star and the lights started to flicker and the door started to open and close and Connie felt a chill of breath and she knew that it was very close, and started to speak to one of them and asked what do you wants from them and the whisper said the baby, and the family, but why and then it whisper the baby was born there.

Then Connie heard the low humming and thudding upstairs and thumping got louder and the things were flying and at that moment it attack her and she fell to the ground at moment and out of breath. About a minute later she heard Star and saying please help me I am in a dark place and I am very scared they will hurt me.

Then Connie lost her and said where have you gone and I need to found you now and I don't want them to take you away, and then the flowers fell to the floor and she smell the perfume and said I know where you are and don't move stayed I will be there in a moment.

Connie when into the family room and saw Star standing and said I need to take you away from here and Star said it is too late for me, just go away Connie and I will be fine and Connie said don't give up and I will take to Josh and Lee.

You don't listen what I am saying Connie, I belong here and this is my home, they are telling you lies and comes with me now, before it too late.

Star stood and didn't move and then she saw her face and her expression and it was not her but it was some dark entity and she said leave her alone and let her go now . . .

Connie decided to pull her and but she didn't move just stood there and Connie thought how do I get her attention to leave.

CHAPTER 19

Sinister

The house was getting darker and Connie was not reaching to Star because the forces were going more dark and evil and Star was beyond reach.

Connie was standing and staring and now she was seeing more than she wanted and it confusing her and she was not sure what she was seeing at that moment and then it pick her up and threw her down and now Connie just didn't wanted to stayed in that house and so she walks back downstairs and went toward the door and it were open about five of them they were standing next to her and she had fear in her eyes and she didn't know what would happen next to her. She was like paralyze and couldn't move and Connie didn't want to stayed but it kept her and tried to run but it kept her in the house and she was frighten to death and then she fell to the ground and was calling for help and so Josh somehow heard her and said I please help me.

Do think that was Star, I think that it was her, do you feel, yes she is in the room, are you should, yes I believe it her. Do you see her, yes I believe I do.

Then they heard a whisper and her voice, and then it was a low humming noise, and a whoosh, then they saw three shadows, on the wall.

Then a lot thumping and thudding and loud footsteps coming toward Josh and Connie, and then Josh got a cut and scratches on his back, and Connie, said I got pushed down on floor, and then she got pulled up and drag.

Connie said, it burning, then it lift to the ceiling, and drop off and to the floor then the blood bleed and Josh got up and ran to Connie.

More whoosh, then the flickering, and continue, and then the door hinge fell off and from inside to the outside.

Now Josh and Connie would getting more afraid what might happen next to them and then Connie said don't look back and just tried to leave this time and don't let them catch you and I will stayed and I will beat them and Josh said tried to save Star and yourself, I will I promise.

Josh about to step out and he heard Star calling him and so Josh didn't leave and Connie was very mad and said it was a trick to keep you in the house and you, stayed and now you will be struck.

They will not let you go and they will somehow get your son Lee.

But Lee is safe with my mom and they will go there and convince your mom to bring the baby back and then they will attack her and even killed her and no one will be safe do understand what I am saying? Loud and clear and you just put us into jeopardy and danger, now you are blaming me and you didn't watched out for Star your friend and now we are paying the price, don't blame me that she decided to go back to the house and well you are a psychic, and you didn't warn Star and I just saw the vision when she step inside the house and I did tried to called her but she didn't answer the phone and okay.

So what are we going to do next? You will come along when we search for her and the next thing will do a séance and then I will tried to reach her and found her and what then?

One thing hope that she is not dead, do think that they killed her?

So far I don't feel it and so I think she is still alive and then she said don't you smell the perfume, is it her?

Yes I think it is and she is very close to her and she is fighting for her life and I don't know if she is strong enough to get back, you need to help her and I know she is my best friend and this creepy house is taking her away from us.

Now they hears footsteps approaching toward them and then Josh got push and pull and drag away and Connie was trying to pull him back and it was stronger than she and but somehow Josh got stronger and got loose and got free and then the phone rang and it was his mom and saying that I am coming over now, and Josh said no stayed home and the phone got static and she hung up and now we have a big problem, my mom is coming and we need to stop her, and but how I don't know.

They will make her comes in with Lee and then they will steal him and they will attack her and she will be harm and maybe killed.

Josh you need to listen to me that you need to meet your mom outside and stop her not to come in and when Connie said that one of the dark shadow attack her and she said run out now and don't looks back and he said I cannot leave you behind save yours son and yourself and your mom.

I will and then he heard a car drove up and she parked the car next to Josh car and step out and when to the backseat and took out Lee.

CHAPTER 20

Séance

The moment that Lee was out the car, Connie did the séance and said let Star go and let her be with her family, you can have me instead and then the breeze and the ominous sound and the eerie in the air and now more heavier got in the house at that second Connie saw the reflection of Star and she was like waving " goodbye" and Connie had a bad feeling that Star was dead, but then thought they were playing with her mind and then Connie said if you hear me Star, touch me and let me find you and I can save you and then the candle when out and she saw her for a brief moment and she was gone.

Meanwhile, Josh stop his mom with Lee and she said his mother is calling him and he must be with her and started to act a bit violent toward him and he said what wrong with you, mom?

She started to approach him and wanted to hit him and shove him down the stairs and grab Lee out of his arms and but Josh just didn't let her get him.

Connie said, they are controlling her and she does not know what she is doing and she need to reach her and she is in a dark place now, and the poltergeist is controlling her and I see it clearing.

Why don't you stop the séance and maybe we can help my mom and she said it is too late, they are all in the room and they want you and your son and then a moment later, that Josh mom was pushed out of the house and Josh said, should I go after her? No don't break the circle and we are fine, how do you know I just know, but hold on to Lee tight and don't let him go.

Then the appearance of Star and she hold out her hand and said I want to hold Lee in my hands and Connie said it could be a trick and be careful and don't give to her, well she is Lee mom.

Josh didn't listen and he just broke the circle and Connie said what have you done, I cannot stayed now, I am leaving and but it somehow pull her up and she was gone. Josh called out to her and nothing, then he took Lee out of her hands and ran out of the house and toward his mom car and got inside and put Lee into the car seat and called out to his mom and said get inside and I am leaving and so she got inside and Star was looking out of the window and was calling out to Josh, and saying don't leave me behind and Josh heard that he left the car and when back inside, Josh mom drove off with Lee and didn't look back not at all.

That night Josh saw Star for a long time and she took her hand toward his hand and walks him into the bedroom and Josh just smiled to see her.

Then Star took him to bed and she lay next to him and Josh was holding on to her and then Josh saw her face and it was not like she was not alive but dead.

No, I cannot believe that you are dead, and she looks and said in soft voice, I am alive and can you feel me and he nodded his head and said yes.

Once again he looks and she had her lovely smiles and he kissed her lips and holds her and she said you need to bring Lee back and we are a family.

I will in the morning and Star slept to him and he thought she was really there and the next morning he got up and she was gone and he looks around and no sign of her, and he called out her name, Star.

About one hour later he heard footsteps coming toward him and a lot of humming and humping sound and more eerie in the air.

Now the house was mores darker and heavier that he couldn't breathe and couldn't move at that moment, and he knew that he was about to be touch by a ghost and was not sure if it was pleasant.

Then he heard Star comes to me and I want you and he follow the voice and it took him into the basement and he saw her toward the wall and she was still and she didn't move at an inch and he said are you okay?

Josh got closer and closer door shuts close and Josh said what going on here? Then he saw Connie face and was whisper to go and don't stayed, do you know where you are? In the basement and they will killed you and Josh said.

How do you know? Well I am one of them now and but I am the good guy and I want to save you and Star, do understand?

Yes I do and just tried to get way and he said I am not going alone and I am taking Star with me, fine if she can leave the house of course.

What do you mean? She could be dead, you're the psychic.

That true I am psychic even afterlife, so you are saying you are dead?

CHAPTER 21

Nightmare begins

Suddenly Josh woke up and looks around and Star was next to him and then she woke up and said what happen? He said I had a bad dream, I should say had a nightmare and you were dead and so was Connie, and she said we are not dead and we are alive and we are in our home, and then Lee started to cried and said Star got up and said I will be right back and at that moment, Josh fell asleep and then somehow he woke up and thought it was Star next to him and it was something cold and he looks and got up and ran out of the room and almost knock down Star and she said what wrong? I thought you were in bed but you were not, and it was a ghost, there are no such thing like that's Josh and Star was skeptic about it and didn't believe what he was saying and one night Josh went out with his friend and Star was alone with Lee, that night Star started to feel some eerie sound and thumping sound and ominous and a lot of chill in the air and then it hit her face and it was a bit scratcher and cut and some blood and then Josh came home said what happen and she said nothing I just hit the wall, and so he got ready to bed and Star sat with Lee her son and they watched some TV and it started and it was the TV was on and then it turned off and but she still didn't think it was supernatural so she lay her head down on the pillow and then she felt an chill and a whisper and she thought it was Josh.

Then Star got up and took Lee into the crib and now Star felt that she was being watched and follow and so she called out to Josh, but Josh was fast asleep.

Star took Lee to the crib and his toys were scatter on the floor and she pick them, up and place Lee into the crib and turned off the lights and when into her bedroom and close the door and Josh was snoring way and then she saw black flies buzzing and so she started to killed them but they came back to live.

Star was going to wake up Josh but then she change her mind and when into the bathroom and looks into the mirror and she saw the reflection of that ugly man with the black hair and long beard and sharp finger nail.

She was going to yelled out but then he was gone and then she turned off the lights but meanwhile the camera were taping and so she said, I will looks at them in the morning with Josh, and she went into bed and place her head on the pillow and it was about 1:54 am and it just was silent on day of November.

Now it was about 3:15 am the house alarm went off and Josh was in a deep sleep and Star woke up and tried to wake him up but not a nudge, and he turned around and slept and Star when into Lee bedroom and he was standing and looking at the wall and crying his eyes out and so Star pick him up and took him into her bedroom and sat on the rocker chair and sang to him.

About half hour later, Josh woke up and said don't hurt my family and Star heard it and said tell me about your nightmare and I need to know and I do want to help you.

Josh was trying to say that they are going to get killed but he didn't say anything and said I forgot what I dreamt and Star said don't lies to me and he said., I am not lying., and he looks at her and said stayed with me and she said I will

Star said I am not going to wait for it too attack us so I am leaving tonight and I believe that is the right decision and by staying,. We will end up dead like the other family and Josh said now you sound paranoid and so you need to calm down and our family will be fine, take my word.

But you are saying that you have nightmare and you wake up in a sweat so I think that I will take your nightmare and they are serious and I think it is not a joking matter and we should go now.

Take it easy, Star it is just a bad dream, yes but peoples were killed in this house and it does have some kind of activity in the house and it going to hurt us and might even killed us and you want to take a chance with our son Lee?

No, I don't but you can go and I am going to proof that there is nothing in the house and you are crazy Josh.

But I am not scares and I will be fine and when you come back in the morning, I will be making breakfast for all of us.

Please come with us and I am begging you and I don't want to lose you and he laughed and said you won't lose me, those were his last word.

Star pack her bag and left the house and Josh stayed in the house.

About a minute later Star came back and said come with us now, and he shook his head and said no.

Star left the house and when inside the car and put Lee in the car seat,

CHAPTER 22

Ghostly haunting

The morning approaching and Lee and Star drove back to the house and sees how Josh was and so she parked the car in the driveway and she took out Lee and when inside in and close the door and she smell the bacon and the eggs and she thought it was Josh, so when into the kitchen and he was not there and the table was set and she sat down and put Lee in the high chair.

Then she took a dish and placed the foods on the dish and then she heard the shower going and she said Lee I will put you into bed and then she when into her bedroom and then low humming and the heavier in the air, and she felt that she was being watched.

Star called out Josh where are you? But nothing and the lights started to flicker and now Star was hearing footstep and they were coming closer and Star didn't know what to do at that moment, she was not sure if it was her husband or a ghost.

Star looks around and she saw a shadow and now she thought maybe it was like a car came by and it was not a ghost.

Then she heard some creaking sound from the floor and saw a man standing and then Star was about to pick up Lee and run of the house and Josh said what wrong, like you sees a ghost, why didn't answer me?

I didn't hear you and so I just came to you, so are really here?

Comes close to me and feel me, and Star said I am sure about that's right now.

Josh said, I am not a ghost and I am alive like you and she slowly when close to him and said do you smell that's? Do you smell the smoke and the roses perfume in the air in the house and Josh said yes I do.

Then Lee burst crying and Star pick him up and said I came to see how you were doing in the house and I am not staying here, and too scared to be here.

Don't leave me and I don't be alone here, Star, and Star said I cannot stayed do you hear what I am saying and I am too terrify to be here.

Josh said you listen to your friend, Connie and she told you that we live in a haunted house with a lot of ghosts and you did love this house and why don't like it now? I am not going said Josh, and I am going stayed, they are tricking you and you are under there spell.

Star tried to convince him to leave but he were move a nudge and so she got Lee and got the bag and was about to walk out of the house and it were not let her go and now Star said I am stuck with you and Lee and I do want to get out of here and she heard whisper and footstep and Josh said we will be fine and we need to have a positive attitude to fight the evil.

What are you saying that we have evil forces in the house, we need to bless the house with the holy water that the priest left about a month ago and get the crucifix and the crosses and we will says prays and they will leave and Star said that we should use sage and lit it and have walks around in each room with the sage and the holy water and do you have the bible, and Josh said yes I do and let do cleanse the house and we will be fine, and I promise that we will be safe.

But I need to hold on with Lee and I cannot let him alone and Josh said yes hold on to Lee and we I take the holy water and we need to get the paranormal investigate to see if they can help us and your friend the psychic to come back to the house and Star said well Connie refused too comes back with the bad vibes that she got last time that she came with me and she said never again,

About a moment later, Josh and Star saw a lot of things and Josh said did see that's and she nodded her head and said yes I did.

But what was it and she said it was a partial ghost and it looks evil and like would harm us and I don't want to be hurt and Josh said I do understand and it will not let us go and so I don't know what to do?

Then Star cell phone rang and she answer and no one was on the other end and Star said it unknown and who calling me, and she looks up at the ceiling like someone was about to pull her up and Josh hold her tight but her hand got loose for a second and then he grab her tight and Lee was near her shoulder and then it happen, it grab Lee and was about to take him, and Josh ran quickly and Lee was safe and he looks around and Star was gone and vanished in thin air.

Josh was calling out her name and Lee was crying and look up at the ceiling and Josh looks and it's was liked bloods from the bottom to the top it was blood and Josh scream out and said why have you taken her away from me?

CHAPTER 23

Taken away

Why have you taken from her away from me and she was my life and now she is gone because you left me with me in this house and what do you have plan for me and my son? Give her back to me, and we will all; stayed in this house and then he saw that dark shadow and coming closer to him and then stop!

Josh looks into his face but he didn't sees his eyes and Josh was stunt and then was like frozen and then Josh got knock down and but couldn't get up and he was out of breath and Lee was crying in his crib and Josh somehow got the strength and got up and ran up to his son and then dark shadow follow him and when he reach is son, he heard Star voice and saying take our son of his house now.

Josh pick up Lee and went to the rocker and sat down and once again a soft whisper in his ear and Josh said I hear you Star tell me where you are?

Then he heard a whoosh and thumping and thudding and things started in emotion and Josh didn't know what to do, and he just ran out Lee room and when downstairs and almost fell and then Lee stop crying.

They got to the bottom of the steps and the door was about to close and Josh just make it on time and one thing before he left he said, I will be back Star and I will save you and I am not abandon you.

Josh got step out and ran for his life with Lee and got into the car and drove off and didn't looks back and then is cell rang and it was Connie and she said you don't have too much time, you need to go back to the house, and Josh said, well first I need to protection Lee, and she said I know . . .

Then Josh hung up the phone and drove like a crazy man and took Josh to Star mom house and didn't trust his mom and he was like possession and he didn't want his son to end of dead.

When he drop Lee and Star mom asked how Star and he just didn't says a word and just left Lee and got into his car and he was gone.

Meanwhile Lee was crying and looking at the ceiling and he was seeing things but Star mom, didn't notice anything and then she heard Star voice saying save my baby from the evil and then it fading away.

At that moment that she had a bad feeling about Star and then she called Josh and said I want to speak to my daughter and he said not right now what wrong?

When Josh arrive to the house and he park the car and open the door and he felt the chill and then another car came and it was Connie and called out to Josh and then she saw the blood on the ceiling and she said that is not a good sign and she said you better go!

Josh refuse and said I am not going until I found her and don't you understand what I am saying Connie, well you are stubborn and you never listen but just take my advice we are all in danger, we are, so be it.

You need to stay near me and not going on your own do gets what I am saying and Josh said yes I do and then she said, I going to called the Mrs. Warren to help us out with this haunting, and she can tell us what going on what kind of ghost that we are dealing with.

But tonight we are alone and I will call her in the morning, so do think that she will help us? I do believe that she will.

Then she said don't you feel the chill and the eerie and ominous sound and creaking and thumping and it is not too far and footsteps and then the orbs floating over our head. There are many ghosts and even shadows peoples in this house because of a lot of tragedy and murders in this house and the reading of a lot of negative.

What are you saying exactly well you bought a haunted house and they are earthbound ghosts and they didn't go to the lights that what I am saying but we need to convince them to go to the light, about Star?

I don't know what happen to her and she's loss a lot of blood and she could have been attacks by the ghost and even killed.

Stop saying that Connie, I need to find her and I don't want to lose her and I do love her very much and how will I raise my son without her.

I don't have any answer but we need to light a candle and says pray for the loss souls.

Do you have the holy water and bible and the crucifix and crosses, I do and we will do cleanse and we will get rid of them, take my word.

CHAPTER 24

Earthbound

Connie started to bless the house and hold on Josh hand and said it will be a little critical and I don't know if it going to work with these ghosts because they are angry and they don't know where to go.

So you are the psychic, so do your thing and then we will be safe to live in the house, and that what I want for my family and I do want Star to be back too, I totally understand but if we are dealing with Poltergeist, it will be a bit more difficult and do you understand and I still think that you should leave and he said I am not leaving my house and no ghost will scare me.

Like Josh, she must have thought the occupants of the house were either dead or seriously hurt.

The sound of breaking glass edged it like jagged lace.

Dead people put on weight it seems to me; both in flesh and our minds, they put on weight.

Then we were finally stopped all tangled together in the middle of the house, and I got out too see how badly they were. I tell you. I expended to find them both dead".

Well she was looking up to see—me____ cawing up. You'd say_ and the sun was full in her face, I remember thinking, holy shit.

She's sonar break like glass if I cannot stop, I see her.

The woman over there she was dead, and I'm pretty sure Connie knew it . . . but she had her straight in the eye.

There was a loud bang, and crumping sound from the attic, Connie, I couldn't drown a breath.

I got out too see how bad they were. I tell you, I expected to find them both dead.

Neither of them was dead.

Of them was even unconscious although, Connie had three broken rib and a dislocated hip from the fall, and Josh said are you okay?

Connie was screaming that she was hurt they were both hurt, wouldn't somebody help us?

We are not alone and there known one will help us.

I see dead peoples standing near us we are surrounded, by them.

What we are we doing to do? I don't know but I need to tell you something about Star, ok I am listening, go on . . .

"She told me a lot of stories"

"Good ones?"

I'm going to miss her so much" me, too" I said, Connie . . . listen . . . I know you were favorite friend, she never called you, maybe she missed a period or was WHOOPSY in the morning? You can tell me.

But she didn't. Honest to god.

Was she WHOOPSY in the morning, yes she was.

"I"LL be, all right" I Said.

He nodded. That's what we say, anyway, isn't it?

We?

I feel pain like anyone else.

I need to touch and be touched.

But if someone ask me, Are you all right?"

I can't answer no.

I can't say help me.

The combination of heat and grief had made me feel as if I had been living a nightmare for the last few days, but that got through.

"And be careful"

CHAPTER 25

Death

There had to be a scrubbing after a death, she said, even if death did happen in the house, itself.

Don't tell me that Star is dead?

My strength was robbed by grief. If the bed hadn't been there, I would have fallen on the floor, don't blame yourself.

Star lying that amid the dust kitties, a stranded of cobweb from the bottom of the box spring and caressed her cheek like a feather.

Her long blonde hair looked dull, but her blue eyes were dark and alert and baleful in her white face.

I know said Connie.

There was nothing there, of course_ dreams, Never—the less.

I spent the rest of the night, looking for Star, do you understand Connie?

It was a choice, I guess, because there were no—more dreams that night, without Star.

Only the nothingness and sleepless nights,

This is one of the most vivid memories I have so clear, I sometimes feel I could step right into it and live it all again.

What things if any, would I do differently?

"I would wander about that".

Only if we didn't move in this house and she were not be gone, and my son would not be without a mother.

Don't blame yourself she told me that she loved this place and she really loved this house, I know but it took her away from me and Lee.

She had come out her grave to visit me?

She did visit you and she is in the house right now, Josh.

I woke with a muffled cry and painful jerk that almost tumbled one off the side of bed.

I hadn't been sleeping long—the tears were still damp on my cheeks, and my eyelids had that funny stretched feel get after a bout weeping.

I really know what you are going through you need to understand that you need to move out of this house now I want to be near to Star.

You need to go now and don't looks back because you have a son and he need you, and you need to let go now.

I can't.

"No" I said" this continues"

It was the memory of Star had been entirely wiped from my mind.

I miss her . . .

But you need to listen to me, and you must do it and don't argue with me and it is for your own good.

So I am listening and so take my advice and leave this house and go to Lee and I will bless this house and with sage and each room and I will called you when I leave, fine I will go and you need to promise me that you will called me when you get home?

I will.

Josh step out and said bye.

Connie said bye.

Josh got into his car and left Connie alone in the house and she started the holy water and burned some sage and then walks in each room.

Now Connie knew that she was not alone and she knew that there was a presence with her at that moment.

At that moment Connie took out the bible and started her prays and walks and was scare at the same time.

Josh arrival sat in the car and waited for Connie to calls him.

CHAPTER 26

Returns to the house

Josh looked at Connie lying on the floor, rubbing his eyes, smearing blood.

You're using me she looked at Josh, her chest swelling, how?"

I don't know, replied Josh. It just works.

But you—you're different. I can feel it"

He laughed and pointed the cross at her.

His voice echoed through her mind. You're mine, Connie.

Connie froze looking in both directions, sizing up the weaknesses. Her chest pounded. Her throat quivered. She felt caged.

"IT don't feel right"

Josh watched Connie breathe, and then whispered under his breath.

"What's that?" asked Josh. "You got something to say?"

Josh shook his head, keeping his eyes on Connie.

Connie started to shake.

Connie's extremities rattled against the floor and her eyes moved back and forth, as he was approaching her.

Josh turned his head toward Connie. "What wrong?"

I don't know.

What happened?

I don't know, Connie.

"IS she dead?"

"I hope not!"

"But you said no she would not die."

"I said I'm not going to hurt you, Connie".

"What do you mean?" Nothing will not happened to you,

"What are you talking about?"

Josh stepped off toward to Connie, then a crunched beneath his feet.

He turned toward Connie, taking heavy breaths, nearly hyperventilating.

Josh thrust forward, reaching for Connie's neck.

Josh clenched his fists in midair and screamed, I don't care what I do what Josh said!"

Josh stuck out his chest and fixed his eyes on Connie.

"Connie got up and ran out of the house".

Connie gagged, straining her breath. She heard him yelling in her mind, "You bitch!

I'LL kill you!

I'll cut your head off and throw it in the basement"!

Connie smacked him in the face, still straining to breathe, reaching, stretching for his eyes, when finally latched on. Her fingers grabbed his ears and thumbs pressed into Josh eyes.

He tried to outmaneuver her, turning and twisting his neck, but she didn't let go.

She dug in deeps, squeezing until he screamed agony. Her thumbs curled inside his eyes sockets, forcing his eyeballs to pop out.

"Are you crazy"? Said Josh to Connie.

Josh looked at Connie, then felt a sharp pain in his neck and sunk to the ground.

Josh lost his balance and fell backward, tripping over Connie, screaming and running his hands over his bloodied face.

Connie hopped off the steps, dazed, gasping for air. She took a few deep breaths and watched Josh crawling on his knees. She kicked him hard with her heel. His jaw twisted to the side and he flew backward, tumbling to the floor, reeling in pain.

She seized the moment, reached deep into his pocket and grabbed the keys.

CHAPTER 27

"Voices of the dead"

She opened her eyes and saw Star kneeling beside Josh. He was desperately trying to stop the stream of blood that was squirting through his fingers.

The blade stuck in Connie's neck at full depth.

Josh stared, sobbing. He took heavy breaths and whispered, "You said no killing.

You promised". He turned to Connie. "We agreed. We promised that no one would get hurt". He wiped his tears, smearing blood across his eyes, and pulled the knife out, covering the wound until the flow of blood had run it course.

Josh cried until Connie took her last breath.

Star stood still staring in shock.

Josh lifted her head, sniffing. "I'm sorry, Connie. You can go now".

Connie began to weep from the stress. She dropped to her knees, trying to make sense of what happened.

Moment later she looked at Josh with confusion. She studied his features, his broad shoulders, his blue eyes, and that moment realized what had transpired.

She felt her face and knew that something had gone wrong.

Josh stood up and Star's limping body rolled to the floor. Josh reached his hand toward Star. She gripped his fingers and rose to her feet.

"Here, said Josh, gently taking the keys from her hand. He fumbled with the keys for a moment and then handed them back to her one.

Connie accepted the keys and silently nodded.

"Call the police, said Connie. I'll stay with him. He wanted to help me".

"But his eyes," How did he control me? Why did he feel so, evil?"

"That wasn't my fault.

I found a Ouija board in the attic and we didn't some things we shouldn't have done. The board told us what would did some things we shouldn't have done.

The board told us what would happen.

It said I'd become a monster and Josh would fix me. We were never the same after that. My face started to deform and Josh's eyes turned Purple.

That's where his power came from.

It was always dark, always sinister.

I knew that, I needed to fix me.

I never imagined we'd spend our life like this.

I don't think he wanted to fix me. I think he wanted to keep his power.

I think he needed me to stay like this because he was afraid if he fixed me, lose his ability to control . . ."

"Control what, Josh?"

Josh looked at Connie with twisted brow and said, "You better go".

"Okay," said Connie. She turned around and wondered what would become of Josh, as she headed for the door.

"Connie?"

Connie looked at Josh. What?

A couple of hours later, I left the house around two in the morning.

I lumbered down the steps and listened to the creaks and cracks in the rafters caused by the whistling wind. Believe it or not, I enjoyed the sounds coming from the rustic structure. I peered toward the car.

I looked around and didn't see anything unusual.

I listened carefully, trying to make sense of it all. The squeaks and groans seemed to becoming from every direction.

Then, something curious happened. I'd hear sounded like footsteps coming toward the car.

My heart, as you can imagine, hammered in my chest, nearly bursting through my rib cage. I looked at the reflection in the mirror to see.

CHAPTER 28

Ghost Whisperer

This wasn't a quiet, don't let them hear you" whisper. Oh no!

This was an "I'm not presently living dimension, so I'm screaming at you" type whisper.

"No. No way," said Josh, shaking his head. "That can happen."

"I think you're right," said Josh, returning to the house was a big mistake".

Josh looked at Connie with brow and said, "You better go."

"Okay," said Connie turned around and wondered what would become of Josh as she headed for the car.

"Connie?"

She turned.

I lumbered down the steps and listened to the creaks and cracks in the rafters caused by whistling wind. Believe it or not, I enjoyed the sounds coming from the rustic structure. For a moment I imagined sprawling out into its cushiony spread, but heard a strange noise coming from the backyard and my skin felt like melted off my face.

I looked around and I didn't see anything unusual.

The stairs opened to the front door, back door and basement door.

I listened carefully trying to make sense of it all. The squeaks and groans seemed to be coming from every direction. No big deal, I thought.

It's just a door. Get over it and fall asleep.

One at a time, I'd hear what sounded like footsteps rolling across the wood floor, carefully pressing down, trying not to be heard. My heart, as you can imagine, hammered in my chest, nearly bursting through my rib cage. I looked in the mirror to see if there was anyone behind me, but I didn't see anything. Then when this thing, whatever it was, pressed on the floor left next to the couch, I couldn't take it. I sat up, turned up head toward the open space and heard a voice, forcefully whisper," Hello!"

This wasn't a quiet, "don't let them hear you" whisper. Oh no! This was an " I'm not presently living in your dimension, so I'm screaming at you" type whisper.

I panicking, jumping straight up like scaredy-cat that I was. nearly falling off the couch.

As I turned I saw a dark shadow, adding to my terrifying experience.

Minutes later, I realized that the shape beside me was only a night stand, but that didn't make me feel better. My heart continued pounding like a jackhammer.

For no less than fifteen minutes, I felt an electric energy buzzing through the house.

I felt as if something hovered over me, almost ear to ear, staring at me.

I peered through the corner of my eye but I couldn't see anything—nothing physical, anyway. But I knew in the deepest part of my house that something was there.

My eyes searched for movement but found nothing. I did see, however, a shadowy figure moving from left to left into the reflection from the stove door.

It was the strangest thing. There was no ceiling fans spinning or curtains, waving.

Everything stood still—everything except the still shadow.

Still, the energy followed me.

After several hours of fighting my fears, I finally relax.

The next morning, I woke up smell of bacons and eggs and sound of coffee percolating in the kitchen. Star and friends, like myself, were shuffling their feet like the undead, trying their best to navigate with squinted, red eyes. We eventually sat down to eat.

In the moment of silence, Star, my friend's wife, asked heard anything during the night. I looked curiously and asked why? She said, "Because someone was tugging at our doorknob off and on for about two hours sometime around four in the morning.

She thought we had mistaken her room for the kitchen, but she been too tired to get out of bed.

She also said that at one point in night felt like someone was sitting beside her, but she was too scared look.

After she told her story, I shared my experience. I affirmed that I never left the kitchen until I ran upstairs and that I never walked toward their living room.

Some of visitors claimed she was a gently ghost, curious, and only troublesome.

CHAPTER 29

Low humming sound

The fire licked the shadows and illuminated the darkness, while she reclined her chair, pulled her leather purse that her eyes, and gazed at the stars.

After a busy spring, she's finally found time to relax with family on Hawaii trip.

At thirty-six, Josh had it all: an attractive fun loving wife, one energetic son.

After putting Lee to bed, Star, his wife stepped down from the kitchen, carrying sodas.

Josh smiled at her.

Star handed his bottle. "I told you we'd have nice time, didn't I?"

"Yeah, but something doesn't feel right. I'm not feeling your intuition this time.

Josh pulled Star onto his lap. She plopped down and kissed him, playfully.

Hey! I know what I'm doing"!

Star wrapped her arms around him and said, "Nice try, Josh. You don't have to impress me. I know you're good with your hands".

The wind blew through the house, sending a chilly breeze through the house.

The house door creaked and Josh turned to see Star jump down and ask, who was that sweetie?"

"Creepy".

Josh said there's a thunder storm warning".

Star stepped toward Josh, crossed her arms as her tracked toward Josh.

Star peeked at the darkening sky and said," " We should get some sleep in case the weather turns."

Their senses felt a drop in temperature and magnetic pulse, warning them of the lurking danger.

Above the attic, a blue flash silently illuminated the darkness.

He heard something else over the roar of the wind-buzz of listened.

A light flashed past the front door. Seconds later, he heard thumped on the living room, followed by a now-familiar voice.

He said something about rumbling!"

"The rumbling?" she covered her head with a blanket.

Her voice muffled,

Star scanned the room, and saw an old woman sitting on the rocker chair.

The lighting flared and exposed another body sitting on the floor. He wore a plaid shirt and torn jeans and cowboy boots. His chin pointed down and his eyes reds searching.

He turned toward the plaid man who was pulling his shirt off, his black, thirty-something beard, long hair, and scar that stretched from his left ear to his left chin.

The man stood up and proclaimed, " My name's Steve.

A rumble shook the earth and the door burst open, startling Josh.

A loud rumble interrupted him and shook the glass and the ceiling fells.

He stopped talking and—wait a minute."

Star looked at Josh. "That's weird."

It's all right boy, insisted Josh.

Lighting struck, the earth trembling and the walls rattled.

A dark foreboding ran through his veins-snarling was unnatural vicious.

"I had a creepy story".

"The Rumbling is based on that experience.

"The old man's laughed his rotten teeth and stirred a knot in Josh's stomach.

He shot out another spit, shared at Josh moment, and then hopped on the couch.

CHAPTER 30

Silently illuminated the darkness

The rumbling began peacefully enough, soothing Josh's soul with a gentle sprinkle. The first gust blew over the house and the door began clatter as rain intensified. Tree limbs and leaves began to tap against the house, warning the occupants as they dreamed of river and rain.

Josh tossed and turned, until his subconscious could no longer take the screaming wind and exploding thunder blasting in his ears.

He sat up and listened. He heard something else roar of the wind—the buzz of the car.

A light flashed past the back door. Seconds later, he heard a pounding thumping on the back door, followed by a now-familiar voice.

He watched Star hold the terrify child in her arms. Her worried eyes looked back at him, begging him to respond—the protection his family.

His mind raced with ideas.

"We could make a run for it. We could drive away.

His thoughts were interrupted by the rumble. Her teeth chattered and the earth shuddered from within. At that point, Josh knew the rumbling didn't come from the lighting or thunder. Is this some kind of strange phenomenon?

"What happening?"

Crash! A lightning bolt flashed outside, followed by a loud and rustling in front of the house. Light beamed into the bedroom and nearby branch landed in front of the house, smashing into the roof and blocking the back door and window.

The dangling fixture flickered and the wiring sparked in a flash of light.

"What's wrong with you people? Don't you realize there's child here?

Josh heard something overhead, than glanced up to see flickering flames on the wall. He pointed toward the wall, where the damage light had sparked.

"The house's on fire!"

Josh scanned the room for a fire extinguisher and saw Connie laughing and Star doddering across the room cursing and searching for Lee.

The rumbling continued and Josh felt sanity slipping away, ebbing out his rational mind, and replacing it with angry disorientation. He spun his head in all directions, furiously scrutinizing the madness that surrounded him.

"Mommy, Mommy! Make it stop! Make it stop!" shout Lee.

"Shut up, you little brat!" she slapped him across the face and yelled.

Josh looked at her, shocked. What's going? That not my Star.

Connie saw Josh's vulnerability and slashed again across her creek.

Josh grabbed her face and dropped to the floor.

Connie leaped on top of Josh, and Josh gripped the hand that held the knife.

Their bodies flip-flopped until Connie's hand broke free and plunged her knife forward. Josh stopped moving and grunted and gurgled. His eyes popped open, dizzily accepting defeat.

At that moment, a gunshot boomed and Connie dropped to the floor, and rolling over Josh.

Twenty minutes later, they were gone.

"That's right," he said. His eyes wrinkled with years of morbid memories.

"Just like the rain wash the sky, so do the rumbling' cleanse the earth of worst kind.

Thoughts of Star's malicious intentions raced through Josh's mind.

Connie gripped his hand, her twisted with concern. Josh glanced at the dead wife and back at Connie, and rested his head on the pillow, and suffocate him.

"Then carried him out of the bedroom and threw him into the basement"

Connie screamed,

Sometimes I'd see a shadow, and when I'd look to see who had walked up behind me, no one would be there. This troubled me for the longest time.

CHAPTER 31

Haunting

The feeling was strange. I knew someone was there. I could feeling was a frightening, electrical sensation, like there were eyes all over me. The feeling sent shivers down my spine.

This continued about six month while I did my job, biting my tongue.

But few weeks back, I was chatting with one of my friends, about spiritual matters when she asked me if I had ever had supernatural experience.

No, I haven't experience supernatural before, but since the death of my friends, Star and Josh, that when it started.

Oh I sees, is it guilt that you killed Josh?

No!

I didn't kill him, it was an accident, I didn't mean to do it but he was aggressive toward me and it just happened.

I don't want to talk about it, okay we won't.

I had been wondering if I was paranoid or going crazy.

When she asked me, I told her I wasn't sure and then asked if she had experienced anything. She said yes and proceeded to tell me that she feels like there is something or someone in the kitchen, watching her standing near her in the same remote corner where I'd experienced the entity.

Upon hearing my friend's story, I told her mine. We went to the kitchen to corroborate our experiences, and, sure enough, we were talking about the same place and the exact same sensations.

After I revealed this to my friend, I had another experience that I'll share in a moment.

A week or two later, a male friend from a different place approach me.

She was new to our area and was assigned to the kitchen. We had never talked before.

I asked her why and she listened to her story before revealing what I knew.

She told me that, from her first day, she felt something down there.

Then, as time went on, she began to get a sense of who it was. She told me that she believed that the entity is a poltergeist who had died during the construction of the house or who had been much richer than mine. She claimed to have seen a full-bodied apparition and believed he was dressed like old fashion clothes, and that he is not malevolent but feels a need to watch over the kitchen.

And now I'll tell you about my other encounter with this ghost.

One night, I was having an especially strong feeling that I was being watched as I traversed the kitchen. When I approached the area where I usually experienced the creepy feelings, I bent down to make an adjustment to a valve that was near floor level. I made the adjustment, but when I lifted my head, I could see as clear as day, set of shoes and dress standing directly in front of me, and I was the only present.

As I lifted my eyes, I could see what appeared to be a full set leg, then the apparition suddenly disappeared.

As you can imagine, this totally freaked me out. I ran around the corner and headed toward the back door.

When I continued to feel the entity's presence, I turned and rebuked whatever it was went downstairs.

I didn't sense anything else for a couple of months after that, but he—if it was really is a he—has returned since then.

Its experiences like this that haves confirmed my belief there is more to this universe than we know, some form of life continues after we die?

Whether you believe in ghost or not, your time here on is short in terms of forever.

She claimed to have seen full-bodied apparition and believed she was dressed like housekeeper worker, and she is not malevolent but feel a need to watch over the bedroom.

CHAPTER 32

Encounter with a ghost

One night I'll was having an especially strong feeling that I was being watched as I traversed the bedroom. When I approached the area where I usually experienced the creepy feelings, I bent down to make an adjustment.

I lifted my head, I could see as clear as day, a set of high heel and red dress standing directing in front of me, and I was the only one present.

As I lifted my eyes, I could see what appeared to be set of arms, and then the apparition suddenly disappeared.

As you can imagine, this totally freaked me out. I ran around the house and headed toward the door. When I continued to feel the entity's presence, I turned and rebuked whatever it was and went downstairs.

I didn't sense anything else for couple of months after that, but she—if it really is she—has returned since then. I have also heard from a third night.

Connie put her hands under her pillow and bunched it up so the sides covered her ears.

You can't handle what's coming. No one can".

Connie was frantic now. Her hands were shaking and she rushed out of the room to compose herself.

Connie felt helpless and terrified.

The clock held steady at 4:15 seconds away from that Connie had warned about.

The gurgling continued.

She was in the kitchen she caught sight of the mist.

Connie took tremulous steps toward the window above the door.

The fog was thick enough, couldn't see anything in front of you.

It crackled and coursed along metallic objects, giving shape to things lost in the mist.

Then she saw a woman lean out from behind the tree. The fog too thick to see any details, but the stranger was very short and medium and she retreated back behind the tree as soon Connie saw her.

She heard heavy, footsteps walking across the floor downstairs, headed down the living room to my bedroom.

Connie stopped staring out the door and ran out.

Didn't looked back when she went outside, but then thought, I need to get back into the house what wrong with me?

The front door opened.

Connie looked do I dare to stepped inside the house?

I do have the strength to go back inside the house?

Connie visibly deflated, and she looked nervous as she continued to walk inside.

"I understand. I really do, but will you just listen to me.

I don't even remember it well anymore."

Connie knew it was a dream. The best one was always were.

And she wasn't hurting anybody, not really.

Her eyes shot open and she realized she was going over backwards.

She tried grab for the chair, but it was too late. In an instant she was on her back, a pizza now decorating her white tee shirt.

"Shit man!" she spat out.

But she cries were drowned out by laughter.

She struggled to her feet, reaching out for a helping hand where none were to be found.

I could've got hurt!

Connie just left the room and just when into the living room and sat down on the couch and put on the TV, and relaxed.

About one hour later, heard humming and then heavy footsteps coming toward Connie and now Connie was scared.

The sights, sounds and smells, she was not alone.

The peoples who came though those doors were ghosts.

She had never been sure if it was because of some weird incident in the house.

Ghost had lashed out at Connie.

CHAPTER 33

Apparition, Demons

She's cautionary tale; a vision reminder of her ability to control herself.

Dangerous places like being in a haunted house alone.

With the creaking on the floors and walls, and a lot of low humming sound thudding and thumping, through the house.

Connie had to deal with it herself and no one to help her at this time.

When Star and Josh got killed in the incident in the house, and I was trapped and they were not let me go!

I didn't know anyone and I was just alone and seeing the dead.

I cannot leave and it won't let me go!

It is coming toward me and I feel it going to grabbed me and take me away.

Connie says if I just sit and being calm and maybe it won't touch me.

I feel the chill in the air and it just whoosh by me and I felt something on my shoulder at that moment. Then it was gone, and I was relief.

About one hour later it happened again and I think it was the dark evil demon.

Demons came close to me and hold me down and I couldn't move and screamed out.

I couldn't see his face and it was like he was faceless and no eyes.

He was tall and medium but no express on his face, and it was cold.

She murmured something under her breath and turned away.

She trembling and fell to the floor with tears of fear in her eyes.

That moment Connie got up somehow and got way from the demons and she ran out of the door and closes it behind her and now she felt she was safe for now.

About half hour later, Connie stepped back into the house and looked around and she felt no heavier at that time.

So Connie sat down and then got up and decided to go into the kitchen to make some hot tea, and she saw the chairs on the table and the pot and pans on the floor.

Then Connie picks them out and removed the chairs from the table and places them on the floor and then she sat down for a second.

Then someone touch her shoulder and it was that demons, and now she couldn't move and she felt violet and assault by the demons.

She turned back and he was gone.

She didn't seem to see anything clearly; she wasn't even sure what happened.

Her eyes glittered a bit, maybe from the tears, maybe from the offer from the ghost.

Connie impression was terrified at that moment.

I couldn't move and speak and at that moment, and I was stunt.

At that time I thought I was losing my mind and the visions were very strong and they warns me to leave, and were be in danger.

Now I knew that I had to get my stuff and get out of here, now!

I got a sign that I were be hurts and harms by the demon that was in this house and I needed to go now.

So I got my stuff together and then the TV when on and off and I saw something on the ceiling crawling on the walls, and that instant I step out and ran to the car and that moment I saw the dark shadow behind me.

I got into the car and I drove away and it was still in my backseat of the car and I seen it in my view mirror in the car.

But I kept going and didn't look back and then I stop and he was still with me and I said what do you want from me?

When, I said that he was gone and I was relief.

CHAPTER 34

Ghost follows me home

Connie got home and placed her stuff on the counter and checks the messages on her phone and it was a weird sound coming from her bedroom.

Connie didn't think much of it at that time and she decided to take a shower and she's undress and step inside the shower and the water was running and then it turned red.

About a minute later she heard something out in her bedroom and she stops the water and steps out and then her shower curtain wrapped around her and she couldn't get loose.

But somehow she manage to break the curtain and fell to the floor and she felt the force pulling her and at that's moment Connie got up and ran out of the bathroom.

Connie was half dressed and just took her car keys and left her place and just kept on driving and somehow she ended up at a cemetery.

She looked back and no one there and she heard whisper and saying her name, Connie, come back home to us.

No, I am home and I am not going back to the house, and I don't belonged there.

For a moment, she actually considered leaving without getting what she thought for a moment, what to do.

Those were the first words she spoken that night, to herself.

The sound of man's gravelly voice sent a shiver up Connie's spine.

"I believe that you could that he is standing near me and give me chill".

Suddenly, an expression of the apparition in front of me!

Shit?

Then apparition reached out his hand and I ran, ran and ran and didn't look back.

She took a deep ragged breath, let it out slowly and realized that apparition was not near me.

At that moment I was relief but still had the fear, that I might get attacked by the apparition.

About half hour later I drove off and drove and drove and didn't looks back and thought I was safe, but then I saw someone in my backseat.

I decided to go back to the haunted house, and use my psychic, and listening what they are saying to me.

To exist in one place, and then the next in a blink of eye—an unfamiliar concept, to be sure, but accurate nonetheless, it sparked the imagination!

Presence, in front of me and I couldn't just walks away, I was frozen and I couldn't move my feet.

Then I saw the apparition standing by my side and then it touch my shoulder and I felt the hand on my shoulder and then it was gone.

I am here.

I am here.

Dissolution, infestation will bring of apparition.

I must survive.

"Before my time," said Connie.

She remembered loud noises and People yelling.

That was the last thing she remembered before seeing the apparition.

Connie spent the next ten days sweating and shaking; having feverish nightmares when she could sleep at all.

"I am taking this seriously" she said.

Connie was grasping air that moment.

She's gone to all the obvious places and not so obvious. She's at her wit end, I am staring at the apparition, right now.

CHAPTER 35

Apparition

"I remember conversation a little differently", said Connie, talking to the dead.

It was not easier to stand up to apparition when weren't actually standing in the same room.

"Oh well . . . excuse me all.

Apparition snapped, slathering and evil laughed.

Connie took a deep, slow breath in and held on. Connie waited to see what would happen next.

She said evenly, breathing out. Leave me alone.

"I probably shouldn't tell you this, said Connie, we are not alone".

Connie looked up at the apparition and anger flashed in her eyes.

Connie felt a knot form in the pit of her stomach, along with a little voices of whisperer.

"Maybe you need lower your expectations."

She wondered if she was seeing the apparition, at this moment.

Once again it touched her and she felt it and then it tried to pull her into the wall.

I am absolutely sure I would have run into danger than the few close calls I did have. However, I also ran across some bumps in that night scared death.

Have no doubt; there is another dimension out there.

I had no idea that I could "see" ghosts. Oh I'd had usual glimpses, thinking I saw someone who disappeared immediately, rubbing my eyes in disbelief. "Hearing"

Someone call my name when no one else was around.

Once in a while I'd have a vivid experience that passed off as surely a dream during the half -a wake state.

Not as easy to shrug off were the times I knew for a fact something woke me from sound of sleep and someone else was in the bedroom with me.

I couldn't begin to count all the unexplained happenings that I made allowances for one way or another.

Then one day, at Josh and Star house, I saw them.

Connie had heard a lot of whisperer and footsteps coming closer once again!

But I knew for fact that they were standing beside me.

Now Connie said this house has as a history, there would murder in this house.

Fact: Twenty people had been murdered in the house or on the grounds.

Many peoples have supposedly experienced the ghosts and spirits at the house.

Some leave and are never heard again.

Connie said what happened to them did they just vanished in thin air?

With the doors opening and closing, locking and unlocking, all on their own, I cannot explained that's!

But I am not going stayed, I am leaving now.

At that moment, Connie got pulled and dragged up the ceiling and she was gone.

"The House got dark and no activities and it was silent".

"Five minutes later, Josh and Star, and Lee were in the foyer and just came home".

Star called out to Connie and said where is she?

I don't know and why was the front door open?

Remember, you told her that you wanted her to stay and see if we had any activities in the house, so I guess she left the house and when home.

Star called out and said well, well she must have left.

CHAPTER 36

Psychic missing

Looks her car is here and she must be in the house, so I will looks for her and you can take Lee to bed.

Fine!

"Josh started to search for Connie and he said something is not right!

Two, with this first bit of proof that maybe she wasn't immune to ghosts, her fear heightened. I suppose I should have fearful too, but in contradiction, I was enjoying myself . . . albeit a tad uneasily, since this was all new to me, said Star.

But where is she?

I don't know.

Hope that she okay?

"I cannot find no trance of her' anywhere!

So keep on looking and I will put Lee to bed, and then he said this house smell of death, what?

I don't want to hears that Josh, and just keep looking, and then he said why don't comes into the foyer and I see some blood spot on the floor.

So I will check out the basement and I will not be long said Josh.

"Just be careful".

"I will".

Josh started to walk toward the basement the front door suddenly open like a wind.

About a minute, Josh heard a whisper and calling his name and he said Connie is it you? Then a whoosh and thudding started and he just lost his balance and fell to the floor, and hurt his ankle. His expression in pain and I couldn't help him.

Star was going toward the basement, and she heard whisperer and someone was calling her name out.

I didn't think I was crazy for believing the place to be haunted.

I thought I was nuts because Josh seemed to be hurt and I was just standing on the top of the steps.

I didn't have a conversation with Josh, just "feeling; sick.

Strange things did happen in the basement and I was terrified to go down to help Josh.

Most of the time the door open and closing and the lights flicker for no apparent reason.

Half of which I could debunk by believing it was a change in air pressure when I entered I feel the heavier in the air.

Star goes down to basement and then stop for a moment and felt a cold chill in the air and like someone just when through her.

"I reach out to Josh and pull him up and is in severe pain and he barely can walk up and then Lee started crying and I just let Josh stand still for a moment".

Five minutes I leave and then Josh is back on the floor and I run to him and I feel that someone push me down.

I felt the hand and it when through my body and then it was gone.

About half hour later, I carry Josh upstairs and we reach the top and then I heard a bang and boom, sound.

"Then Lee was crying and I took Josh to the couch and gave him a pillow and I will be right back" and he begged me not to go!"

I was living in fear.

That night I'd been watching Josh and I decided to try to communicate with the ghost.

At that time, I had a name for him. It was not his name of course, but it seemed to suit him.

So many years had passed I've forgotten it now.

Star burst into tears and Josh said what wrong?

CHAPTER 37

Paranormal investigate

I'm ready scared this time. He said he was going to kill me"!

About the time, entry of the door down stairs slammed. From the bottom of the stairs, Josh screamed, what happened?"

Thump, thump, thump echoed up the stairwell as he made his way to our door.

I grabbed the phone and dialed.

Nothing!

It was completely dead.

I tried again.

Still nothing, Star, go to the bedroom and lock the door," I tried again.

The door rattled on it hinges with the force of the first impact, but the lock held.

It seemed he got stronger than the one before, Once again rattled violently.

The third hit sounded as if he'd thrown his massive body against the paneled door.

"Soon the sound of running footstep and whisperers through the door"

"Five minutes it was gone".

"I step out and I felt the eerie and ominous, I was being watched".

Between Josh and the ghost, I had to leave and I had enough.

One day I smell a pipe smoke in the foyer.

I knew I was not alone but it was time to called the paranormal investigate to the house.

When Connie started spending the night at our house on a fairly regular basis, I didn't think much of it much of it.

We'd been friends our entire lives and were prone to doing so.

However, one night it wasn't terribly convenient to have house guest in a haunted house.

Being such good friends, it was easy to explain the situation and ask her to go home for the evening.

Connie's eyes grew wide and for a moment, I thought was going to cry.

I remember, when she said I'm so sorry! Now I remember her sadden.

"At moment I needed to find a paranormal investigate to sees if I have ghosts in the house, and I know that I was seeing shadows and hearing voices".

Now I moved into the narrow hallway to see if it was clear, so I snuck into the kitchen and pick up a phone and made one to the paranormal investigate, about what was happening in the house.

I spoke for a while and then he said that he was coming over with his group.

After I finished speaking to him, I hung up the phone, when to see how Josh was doing.

"Josh was lay down on the couch and but seem like something was beside him, like an orb."

"I was too scared to speak and I just look and it was still in the room, and I just walk over to Josh, and I said it here."

What here?

"GHOSTS"

Then Star said, the paranormal group is coming over in half hour and we will leave the house when they investigate the house, and Josh nodded his head.

"About one hour later they arrive to the house and Star let them in and shown them where the most activities in the house, and then they set-up the camera in every rooms, and Josh and Star and Lee left the house that night."

"Star said to Josh is that a good idea that we left them, I think that we should go back, but they told us that they wanted to do it without us."

But I didn't tell them that Connie was missing in our house.

CHAPTER 38

Paranormal investigate at night

One of team rolled her eyes and let me out of this house, and what wrong?

I, cannot stayed, it is taunted me, and I think that we will get hurt here if we stayed.

No, I am leaving, I feel an evil force here and we are not safe, how do you know they are standing beside us.

"This house is haunted".

"What makes you think it's haunted?"

She paused for a moment to think it over, before saying.

"I see shadows all the time.

"What other thing?"

She took her head. I am going crazy."

Several minutes in the house and I just don't like the uneasy feeling about the house.

I know that sounds nuts, but every time I walk through house, I hear whispers.

My face flooded with stress and walk out of the house.

Meanwhile she when inside the van and waited for them to comes out.

Now been hours and no sign of them.

But I still stand in the van and waited and waited.

I looked out and I saw shadows in the windows, and I still stayed put.

I refuse to go inside the house.

This was probably one of the single most ridiculously arrogant decisions I've made.

Solely because I was under the impression I knew getting into.

I did feel uncomfortable, but felt safe in the van.

I knew the house was haunted.

"Meanwhile they started one room and the cameras were set and they did walks through and then things started to happen to them."

"One of them, he fell down the stairs and then one of them got drag a not seen again!"

The presence was very strong in the house that things started to move and been threw around in the house.

The lights started to flicker and the doors and windows started to open and close, and the head investigate, Steve said did you get this on tape to Mark.

Yes I did and so we will do one more walks through and where are the rest of the crews? I don't know said Mark.

Hope that they are okay?

I think they were upstairs and I think that they will be back soon.

I hope so!

Pretty Soon we will be done with investigates of the house and then we will pack it up, I hear you what you're saying.

So Mark you can start packing and I think that we have enough evidence to show Josh and Star.

Meanwhile, in the van, she heard a knock at the door and she said I am not going inside and leave me alone.

Once again a second knock.

"So she opens the van door and it just pulls her out and dragged her out and she was gone".

About half hour later, Mark and Steve were packing and then they felt a whoosh, and then felt something on their shoulder and it was a scratch and blood coming out.

"So what happened? Then they were all gone."

CHAPTER 39

Investigate when wrong

IT was strange. When they came home and saw all the equipment in the house.

Entire room lit with light.

Star, I just saw a shadow shaped like a person, ghoul, or devil.

Now many people in our house, we cannot stay, said Star to Josh.

Because we can be next to be gone.

"What are you saying to me, said Josh?"

"We are in danger in this house don't you hear what I am saying?

With the footsteps and voices, we do have "GHOSTS".

Now, I realize that we are not alone, so what are saying that we should leave.

Come on pack the stuffs and let get the hell of out of this house now.

Any fear is staying here, and so comes on now, I need to pack one more camera, so I will wait for you outside, fine.

I didn't budge and it got stronger and I couldn't get away.

"What's going on?"

About that time, the entry door down stairs slammed. From the bottom of the stairs, he screamed,

Thump, thump, thump, echoed up the stairwell as he made his way out.

Lock door.

"These doors are paper thin; the locks won't let me out".

IT seemed stronger it won't let go.

Soon the sound of footsteps coming closer to me and I had no place to run.

"Yeah, I am fine. Why?"

"Just checking. "Star glanced over her shoulder. "I wish they would come back.

Do you think something could've happened to them?

"I am sure they are around somewhere.

Whatever got them can't still be alive."

What do you think that noise was? Is a ghosts or poltergeist?

Whatever attacked them must been taken away, to the next life.

"What was that?" Star's voice came out octave higher than normal, making her squeal in pain.

They listened for a few seconds. Someone was coming down the stairs toward them.

Star and Josh, but the crackling frightened her. She didn't like being in the house alone.

"Let's move—move now!"

"Okay." Star's voice was less confident than normal.

Star squinted, trying to see off into distance, slowly smiled. "Is there a light head?"

"IT's a light.

Do you see it in the kitchen?"

Yes I do.

"Let's hurry."

Something grunted behind me.

Star turned around and smiled at Josh and look at the top.

Josh didn't answer but ran toward Star. Star stood there and then screamed.

IT wasn't Josh.

IT wasn't even human.

"Run!" Star yanked Star called out Josh.

CHAPTER 40

Unfortunate events

Star sprinted as fast as she can she could beside Josh until her foot slipped on the floor. She tumbled to the floor, almost dragged with the knife toward Josh.

Cuts and bruises scrap her skin, but her body was too numb to register all the injuries she suffered. A shriek ripped from her again when she spotted the demon right behind her.

"Get up!" she yanked Star to her feet and sprinted away from the demon.

How did this happen?

Although she would never admit it, she was pretty shaken up.

Star tried to convince herself that what was happening to her was nothing, like a horror story.

It was just series of episodes of unfortunate events that left her out breathe.

"Then we should go. He said to give him ten minutes, and we waited eleven.

We'll meet him on the main road'.

Star nodded and reached out her hand to Lee, who took it and gave it a gentle squeeze. "IT terribly cold out there, but doesn't feel as bad as it did.

"I know. I guess we're getting used to it. Let me know if you start feeling warm again. That's a sure sign of hypothermia." Star rubbed Lee's fingers" Are your feet still feeling numb?"

"A little, but they're better. And I'll tell you if feeling warm," Star's promised as they carefully made their way downhill. They hiked with little poodle, listening out for Josh would behind them.

She didn't to tell Lee, but her feet were killing her, and she limped. She would never wear those boots again.

"Yeah, I am fine. Why?

"Just checking" Josh glanced over her shoulder. "I wish Star and Lee would be fine.

Star put her arm around Josh and smiled. I'm sure they are somewhere in the house. We can see pretty well, despite it being night.

Star probably wanted to stop again. Besides, that's we are safe now.

Whatever got them can't still be alive".

"She has been slow. I think they would've been with us if they got out sooner."

Star laughed a bit. And Josh was right. Nothing could live that long, but a ghost.

"I think we should been will be well. Star glanced around.

They headed down the gravel road. After a few minutes of walking, a snap, sounding like a branch breaking, in the forest. Star jumped and glanced at him.

Josh didn't answer but ran toward them. Star stood there and then screamed.

It wasn't Josh.

"Run!

"Keep running!" She breathed as she slid down the hill.

"I am!" Star tripped again and landed face first on the ground.

"The fall ripped Star's hand from Lee's grasp. Star lost her balance and rolled head over heels several feet ahead of Lee. Her fingers dug into the rocks, shredding the tips of her nails. She stumbled to get up.

"The ghost caught her son and leapt on top of her. Star's shriek and the sound of tearing voice resonated path.

Star screamed her eyes darting back and forth for some way to fight off the ghost.

Star shook her head to clear her vision.

The ghost howled in pain and dropped its prey only to come after Josh.

The ghost stalked her and grabbed her hand and threw on the ground.

She smelled its fetid hot breath. A scream broke from her.

She wasn't ready to die tonight. IT gripped her tighter, bruising her flesh.

CHAPTER 41

Flesh

Star and Lee were likely dead too. This realization smacked Josh hard and almost knocked him down.

Snap!

She turned and whirl of back toward him.

Then, light struck her.

House lights burned as bright as the sun.

Do you see what I am seeing Josh?

A screech erupted into the night.

Only the darkness she so feared so much remained.

She leaned her arm against, and crunched and seem like her arm was broken.

Josh spoke in a spooky tone and wished he had a flashlight for effect.

She emerged to the forest onto the main road.

She was an innocent victim, except she kept muttering they were all dead.

She also said it was her fault".

Hard rains swept through the area recently making the road muddy.

He lowered his voice and whispered.

At night she screams, claiming a short-man ghost try to kill them.

He turned his head to face the road, almost expecting to see a big ghost here.

The storms must have struck it down.

Tree lined the road on either side, and he knew he couldn't go around it.

Are you sure it was around here?"

She swallowed and looked around the woods, as if a ghost would jump out at them and there.

They continued searching until they discovered the rest of their mutilated corpses. They were laid out in some clearing a few miles away.

"Let me see with my phone" Josh motioned for Star to get out.

Josh went around the other side to help Star climb into back of to the top of the hill. He watched as she held her cell phone up as high as her five feet frame would go. If only it work, she could go back home.

"I have two bars!" She dialed the number.

Then she lost the signal, tried again, but had no luck. "Sorry, you guys," she said, and helped her down and back to him.

We can't be too far from the house.

It shouldn't take Josh more than an hour or two.

It would work out fine.

Star peered into the dark. She didn't want her Josh to go there alone.

"Are you sure you go by yourself?

"We can't wait here. Star's eyes look and wondered what she see out there.

Don't worry about it."

But she couldn't let her Josh go out there in the forest alone. If was very dark.

With a waning moon, they couldn't even count on much moonlight, if any.

Someone has to go, I'm that someone."

The thought of walking who know long in the dark frightened her, but Josh had a point. She finally concealed. "All right, Josh. You go.

We'll stay here and wait for you."

"I think we should stay together, "Star said.

"I don't want to stay here, Star trembled, cold and scared.

"What if Ghost come up here after us.

"No one will coming up here," Josh laughed, although the sound held no mirth.

CHAPTER 42

In the forest

"Star has point, " Josh shrugged. "We don't know that you will make it out of the forest?

But he didn't listen to her, and there was out of Josh walk out there in the dark.

"I don't really want to remain here, but I don't want to walk either.

"No one knows were here," she whispered and looked at Lee.

How dare he's considering us alone here.

"I'm coming wait for me, called out Star to Josh.

You all lost your freaking minds.

No, we are not staying and I feel the strong presence here, and it will attack us, if we stayed. We need to go now, before it too late.

It was so dark Star could barely make it out for two steps in front of her.

She shoved her hands into her pockets. What are we standing around for?

Let move it"!

IT won't be too bad. Three or four miles, right? IT could be even less,"

Star gave her an optimistic smile and took hold of Lee's hand.

A heavy sigh rushed from her lips like a plume of smoke and framed her face in dark fog. She didn't know how long would take them but they might as well get over with.

Star trembled in fear about walking at night. Star was so brave to venture into the forest, especially since she knew her son was secretly terrify of the dark.

She stayed close to her son as they climbed up the road.

The late January night air was so cold her nose was already stinging red, and running after four minutes.

IT was strange walking around the woods at night. It was quiet.

Ghosts wouldn't likely come out, but she couldn't be certain. She rubbed her hands together. Her fingers felt like she'd been holding ice cubes, and her toes were frozen. Blisters formed on her feet.

"I wish I had worn something besides sneakers."

She marched over the gravel road.

"I wonder if any ghosts are out there. " Star stared at the stars. "Here we are in the middle of nowhere, Lee.

Star rolled her eyes and whispered to Lee, what that noises? I don't know.

"I need a moment to rest.

"Hello?"

Star had to smile, Mom, we're stuck out, said Lee.

It cut me off".

"We haven't even walking that long. " Star glared over.

"Let's go".

They plodded along and all conversation ceased for a few moments.

A loud snap broke the silence, and she gave a short scream as her foot slid from under her.

I'm fine. I just slipped." Star regained her balance. "My feet are getting numb from the cold."

She wiggled her toes, trying to bring back circulation.

Star came up beside Lee and grasped him other hand. "You okay?"

Star nodded.

"So what do you think that sound was?" Lee asked.

"Probably a branch falling,"

Star could tell the sound had spooked us.

But she was probably too much of a woman to admit she was scared.

CHAPTER 43

Chase by a ghost.

She paused as if to stretch the suspense.

Star didn't know if she could take it anymore before Lee continued him tale.

They say that it's still out here, watching and waiting. And it's hungry."

They are scattered in all directions.

"You don't really believe that, do you, said Lee.

"We made our way down the hill to the house, and the crept along some GHOSTS in the surrounding so we could get close enough to the house.

Once at the house, we stuck to the walls and made our way around the house until we found Josh.

We took a chance and smashed the lower glass window of the door to get in.

Once in, we walked down a darkened hallway until we reached the interior of the house.

An abandon house was very strange sight indeed. What was the point of all this situation, Josh came along and we were not alone.

"IT just occurred to me, Josh said.

"Our world is overrun by GHOSTS, and they are in this house.

We decided try to find some sort of cameras, thinking that if we get some surveillance and see if we catch something.

I jumped back and thing freaked out spasmodically, banging against the door.

Josh and Star had come into the room by now, and seemed like amused by the fact that I been startled.

"I locked myself in here, the keys are over there on the floor, please let me out . . ."

Ghost looked and sounded eerie, there was nothing there.

I opened the door.

Josh practically fell out of the room, taking a deep breath of air.

I supposed he was right, it is preferable to being torn apart or attack by the ghost.

The room seemed completely intact, but Josh said no one was in it at that time of attack.

I guess there was no reason for those of things to go in if there was nothing at all there.

I felt it would be okay, Josh wasn't acting anything like any of things we had encountered.

We looked over all the doors and windows, surveying the house from strange oscillating eye of the various cameras situated all over the property.

We could see small movements, but most of them were just sitting still: some were rocking back and forth.

One small girl sat in the middle of the room, stoic as a statue, staring at the lens of the camera, at us. IT sent a cold shiver down each of our spines.

Josh glanced at Star who confirmed what Josh had seen, and Star's hand out to leaving the house.

The chain snapped and the door exploded inwardly, clipping the Star's arm, sending her spinning into the foyer. As she fell, now free of ghost, she landed on the floor hard, her head hitting the bottom of the stairs in the foyer.

The force of the open door flying open also had effect on the man, also.

Face was bloodying his nose, and sending him to the floor.

Josh shook of his fall and Star noticed the hand that hadn't been holding the clump of hair in his hands.

Josh's had spun around, eyes flowing Ghost as it disappeared from the foyer.

As he turned his gaze quickly back it was gone.

Josh was screaming.

CHAPTER 44

3:15 am

Josh screamed a loud NO as it all happened, then stood in complete silence as three ghosts stand by Josh in all directions.

Josh tried gurgle out something, but he couldn't make it out.

The access door was on the opposite side, so we stayed close to the front of the house.

As we heard voice from across the way, taunting us, we were terrifies at that moment.

It was coming toward us and it will attack us again if we don't get out of the house now.

We broke into a full run now, more concerned about reaching our destination than being attack.

Once Josh reach the door, Josh opened it and held it open as Star and Lee ran out of the house.

Josh took one quick look back just in time to see three of the ghosts coming.

They locked eyes with each other for a brief second.

"Hey!" yelled one of the ghosts.

Josh's eyes widened and he let go of the door, turned back the way he came and sped away in a full-on run.

The three ghosts just vanished in thin air.

I just waiting to see if they we leaving, will be following us.

The deep aggressive voice came from behind us. We slowly lowered our ghosts over our heads.

One of them grabbed Star forcefully made her physically react.

I wished there was something I could do to escape this situation.

As I walked, I titled my head back with my eyes closed, hoping this was all a dream. I opened my eyes, head still titled, I noticed movement through the backyard, I didn't catch what it was. Something dark had been in the yard and then ducked out of sight.

Then a thought occurred to me. I spoke up.

"What could we possibly want from us?

He felt his way cautiously down the creaking sound and paused there in the darkness. It shifted slightly as he watched.

Josh frowned.

They were familiar to him.

Despite the wind, the air was eerie and spooky.

His words sounded dull and lifeless to his ears, and clamped his mouth shut.

The half-seem oddly unfriendly presence. Even when shone the light on it, he could not escape the feeling that something lurked just beyond the innocent white circle of light in the air in the backyard.

Especially not when he still he still in the backyard, it was spooky.

Josh it time would come when Star leaving would not haunt her, but tonight with the backyard still trembling and creaking in the cold.

The wind screamed, the house rattled on its hinges the door was torn off,

Star knew that she was blamed for Connie disappearance in the house.

Star's it my fault about Connie.

Something warm trickled down her face, she tried to raise her left hand to it, but her arm didn't work; it felt numb and somehow . . . misshapen.

It's broken, Josh thought . . . of all the stupid . . .

And I'm bleeding. The thought seemed to come from within a deep fog.

She tried to stand, using her arm to lever to herself up, but a wave of nausea slammed her back to the concrete, and turning her head he retched out the sour remnants of her late-night snack, and she said no more, I will not do that's!

CHAPTER 45

Haunted House

The shock cleared Josh's head, He knew where he was now, all right: the farthest corner of the basement, right up against the outside wall, not from the wine cellar, a separate room with both a door into the basement and steps leading up to the kitchen.

Josh felt his way along the broken edge of the floor until the wall. Then reaching his left hand, and found an electrical cable, strung from through rusted metal hoops in the crumbling concrete.

As he pulled himself upright, a breath of cold air against the back of his neck goose bumps, and chills.

The breath of cold air came again, curling around the base of his neck, flowing under his face, caressing his face like a hand . . . like Star's hand, last time she touched him, as he expected, but as if saying a sad, disappointed good-bye to all their hopes, all their dreams, all the happiness they'd once promised to bring to each other.

Suddenly became as cold and sharp as a knife.

Pain slashed across his chest like fingernails, and terror followed after, as in the absolute silence that followed his scream, a moment in which even wind died away, a voice in the darkness said, clearly and coldly and utterly calm, "Josh". And the voice . . . the voice was Star's.

He screamed again, a wordless howl, and pain forgotten, scrabbled along the wall for the door to the front door. He found it, tugged at it screamed curses at it when it wouldn't open, and then when it did, so suddenly he fell, crawled back toward it, sobbing and panting.

Inside, he pulled himself up, bottle of wine and bottle crashing heedlessly around him. More of Star's work, those bottles: those times he'd been gone, she'd always said she was making the wine.

But he'd believe her.

She was perfect, too beautiful, he knew how men looked at her—the same way he'd looked at her—knew, knew they had to be coming here when he was away, had pictured their hands on her.

And Star had gone away.

He stepped forward, and broken glass from one of wine he'd pulled down stabbed his hand. Spilled brine and vinegar seared the wound and bought him to his hand. But he crawled forward anyway on his hands.

His lacerated hand found the wooden steps leading up to the outside cellar door at the same moment that the door leading into the basement slammed shut behind him.

The noise brought him back to his feet, his whole body now aflame with agony.

He could feel blood running down his hands, could feel it sticky on his usable hand, but it didn't matter.

He was almost out of the house, now almost up the steps and into the clean, cold wind. It called to him promising to wash away that's nightmares of his own making. Hallucinations, that's all, he told himself as he dizzily mounted the steps.

But I shouldn't feel guilty. I shouldn't. I didn't mean to do it. It was her fault.

She should have come with me. She should have stayed with me all the time.

She lied . . . she never admitted it, not even at the end, not even when I was holding her down, not even when my hands were on her throat, when I was reached up and touched my face. Maybe if she'd admitted it. I wouldn't have . . . but she was lying to me. I knew she was lying. And I couldn't stand it.

Couldn't stand to hear that beautiful voice telling me lies . . . couldn't stand to know that even our lives were torn.

Josh bumped his head on the front door.

The wind died away again outside. Josh found himself holding his breath, listening. Of course it had all been his own imagination, so he wouldn't hear . . .

"Stay with me, Star whisperer in the dark. "Don't leave me alone with the wind, Josh. Stay her with me. Stay . . . forever. And this time there could be no mistaking the ice-cold touch of her hand in the dark . . .

CHAPTER 46

Paranormal entity

"Come on, Josh, it won't be so bad," my wife said, fake smile in place as she slid the key into the lock of the ridiculously huge front door. The old brick house with ivy clinging to it walls looked like something is staring at us at that moment.

With a grunt, my wife pushed the door open and the iron hinges gave a loud creak.

I so didn't want to be here.

The enormous chandelier overhead stirred, sending a creepy tune through the house I now called home. There was dark wood on every wall, and a steep staircase took up to the better part of the entry. My wife would have loved it here, I thought, my heart squeezing.

His Jaw was clenched tight as he had barely looked at me in weeks.

I could hear the music blaring from the house, I stood four feet away, as I watched him, he turned and he was gone.

Like blowing out my eardrums would change the fact we'd moved over but stand there still and staring at me, and I was froze and scared at that moment.

Josh flipped the light on and turned to the entity, and said this is my place, not yours!

And a place like this would have plenty of spirits, which terrified me—because I can see the dead, and have been able for a while—since I loss Star and Lee.

Nothing could take away the pain. I missed my Star and I couldn't understand why I could see other ghosts, but not Star.

In fact, I still can't understand why my wife hasn't "visited" me.

"I got a great deal on the place, "Josh said into thought s.

"I bet you did, "Josh said.

I knew the old house would be full of ghosts.

Maybe this time would be Star.

With my heart racing nearly out of chest, I turned my head and could see the ghosts standing just off the foyer—short figure lingering in the shadows. Disappointment washed over me. It was a woman and not a man.

Not my wife.

I knew better than to make eye contact. Once I did, the ghost never left me alone.

"Why?

Ghost glanced over at me, anger brimming in his brown eyes. There had we'd been close, but after Josh, everything had change.

I cleared my throat.

Anxious to be alone, I headed up the creaking stairs to hide away in my room, praying the ghost didn't follow.

"I blocked out their voices and resisted the urge to take the steps two at a time.

Ghost followed behind me, the ghost fast on her heels.

Forcing myself to remain calm, I took a left at the top of the steps then pushed open the third door on the right.

I wrinkled my eyes. The room filled with my familiar furniture, was huge and smelled musty. There was a large window covered by hideous silver drapes that might just an ancient as the house itself. I noticed two doors, one leading to a closet and the other to my own attached bathroom. Pleasantly surprised, I opened the door. There was a pedestal sink with a mirrored medicine cabinet above it, and the shower with a basic flower curtain hanging from the gold loops.

Though the bathroom wasn't huge but any means, it was mine, and I was glad I wouldn't have to venture into the hallways at night to use the bathroom.

I crossed the room and looked out the only window to find I had a perfect view of the roses on a grassy knoll surrounded by tall trees.

The air around me suddenly turned cold, and I felt someone standing behind me. It's a sensation I'll never get used to, and I feared turning seeing a ghost in the bathroom with me.

CHAPTER 47

Shadow of the night

I saw that ghost. I learned that could physically feel what they time of their death. I couldn't tell what would happen next?

I closed my eyes, willing the ghost to go away. It didn't.

I turned my head to the right to just slightest bit and saw a woman standing directly behind me. She appeared to be a younger than me, with shiny gold hair that brushed her shoulders. Though I wanted to look her straight in the eye, I didn't. I couldn't let on that I could see her.

"Josh "I yelled louder this time

It had been the biggest mistake of my life. The young woman had hounded me nearly every waking hour until finally I ignored her, pretending to no longer hear or see her. It worked, even if it took months for her to realize as much. She never bothered me again.

I told myself I see ghosts.

I brushed a trembling hand though my hair.

I shook my head. "No, I just need a nap"

"No.

As Josh headed for the door, to the bedroom, and been follow by a ghost.

Not too late meant we'd mostly see tomorrow.

"No I'm fine.

I rolled my eyes and ghost giggled like a boy.

Ghost shut the door, and I took a few minutes to pull my black hair. And, I went to sleep.

Needing to clear my mind, I checked to make sure I had everything o needed out of window.

Josh was haunting in his home.

It was almost unsetting not to hear, children playing, and trains and ball bouncing.

I know it sounds weird but strangely comforting to know ghost was on the ground.

A car blew past me, missing me by inches, pulling me abruptly back to the present.

I felt a strange compulsion to run, mixed with an almost need to explore it, but o stayed in the room.

I didn't dare. Honestly, I didn't have the guts. Plus, I didn't come to see ghosts.

My hand shook as I walks slowly back to the room.

Seeing no one, I rolled up my legs of my slack and slid my sock down.

I took a deep, steadying breath, released it and before I could talk myself watched as blood beaded against the knife. I cut further, deeper, and he release came, taking with it anxiety and frustration that had been building within months.

Blood streamed down my ankle, soaking into my white sock.

I was no longer alone. How could I possibly explain what I'd been up to?

Slowly I turned to find a ghost watching me with disbelief in his piercing brown eyes. That disbelief quickly turned to bewilderment as our gazes locked and held.

Oh my God. It was the ghost from the house . . . and he had followed me here.

"You can see me, "the ghost said in a thick wood.

I was so screwed. What had I done? Why had I reacted?

Now every sprit in Star would be my doorstep waiting to talk to me.

Only one person had ever asked me about cutting and had been Star.

"Are you well?" He said concerned.

I pushed away from the ghost, wanting to get as far away as fast I could. Why had cut out in the open? What an idiot.

CHAPTER 48

Ghost encounters

"The ghost followed beside me. " I know you see me.

You looked right at me for feck's sake. Speak to me, Star. Say something"

He was starting to sound desperate.

I rushed from the house, onto the main road, and nearly into the path of an oncoming truck that had to swerve to hitting me.

The ghost stayed with me, and even moved ahead and then she came to an abrupt stop in the middle of the road.

I walked straight through her and smiled inwardly as he cussed under his breath.

She was back beside me in seconds, staring at me.

My footsteps faltered as I come closer to the house.

As much as I'd like to escape to my room and crash out, I couldn't face the inquisitive Star, or for my matter.

I had feeling annoying here wasn't about to leave me alone.

I left the main road and veered off, onto the grass and toward the lake, hoping would get the hint I didn't want her company.

"I have no intention of leaving, if that is what you hoping I will do, whispered in my ear, "I shall stay with you every day until you acknowledge me."

She was so close I felt her icy breath on my shoulder.

A medium car packed with stuff drove away and quickly averted my gaze.

The car sped and I kept walking away from the road, and over a small grassy field.

I found a place on the lake's edge. I glanced over my shoulder to see the house, which gave me some comfort. Not that I felt in danger from the ghost at my side.

She started sing, and I knew she did get under my skin.

Siting on the bench, I leaned over and picked up a few flowers. I threw them into the river, one by one and as promised, the ghost didn't fleeting moment at the cabin when I looked at her.

I couldn't believe how cold she was with long brown hair and brilliant brown eyes.

Given the clothing, I wondered how long she'd wandering the earth as a ghost.

"Talk to me, I swear to you that I will not harm,"

I liked her soft voice and sexy accent . . . even if she did speak like she was beauty queen.

"And if do not speak to me, I will not leave your side . . . ever. I can speak all hours of the day and night, if you like.

Josh better judgment told me to keep my mouth shut, and yet a part of me was curios. I'd never met a ghost close to my age. I ran a hand down my face in indecision.

"Or I can continue to speak or perhaps you singing . . . "

Before I could talk myself out of it, I turned and looked directly at her.

My heart skipped a beat.

She was gorgeous. Her eyes even sparkle and move amazing than I thought.

The brilliant pink orbs were framed by short, thin lashes any girl would kill have, and she had low cheekbones and nice, medium lips. Medium builds and great body.

As I continued to stare at her, her brown eyes mirrored the same shock as when I'd first looked at her.

My name Connie, and yes—I see you'.

"Connie, whispered, her lips curving into a grin that made my thighs tighten.

"Do you know I have not conversed with anyone for over ten years?"

I couldn't even imagine going a day without talking to someone, but ten years?"

CHAPTER 49

Cursed

"Yes, It is. By the way, my name is Josh. "It nice too meet, you, Connie.

"And it's a pleasure to meet you, Josh." She tilted her head slightly as she watched me, and I shifted under that intense stare, wondering exactly what she was watched me, and I shifted intense stare, wondering exactly what she was thinking . . . . especially since she knew my life.

"So how did you die"? I blurted, before she could start drilling me about why I'd been cutting myself.

"I was strangled".

Talk about a miserable way to go. Suddenly, I remembered the way my throat and chest had burned earlier when she'd come into my room. The pain had been intense. "So . . . why would someone strangled you . . . or was it murder?"

My death was murder. A friend who betrayed me to my family is one responsible.

"No I stay here because I am cursed to roam these walls for eternity, Josh said matter—of-fact.

"Cursed?"

I laughed, wondering if she was trying to pull my leg of bullshit, but could tell by the look on her face that she was serious.

I had no idea that curses were real.

Connie gaze lingered on my face, making me uncomfortable. I hadn't even bothered with makeup. When exactly did you die?"

Ten years ago on Valentine day.

My heart missed a beat. You lived in the house?"

Josh nodded pride shinning in his eyes. Yes, I did with my Star, my wife and my son.

"No, I am alone."

How depressing. I couldn't imagine being alone for so one year wandering day after day with one to talk to. And no could see you?"

I had noticed with the young ghost when she came around. At first she would look as human as me, but the longer she stayed, the more her energy began to fade, so did form, until she disappeared altogether. Strangely enough, I didn't want her to go. It was nice to have someone my age to talk to.

His gaze shifted down to my feet. "You do not have to answer me if you don't wish to, but I am curious . . . why did you hurt yourself?

The question to Josh was surprised me, and as uncomfortable as it made me feel, 1 answer her. "I was standing.

"My life hasn't been the same since, and to deal with the pain, that my wife died.

For some reason her desire to understand make me like her.

I took a deep breath and said now I need to rest.

It had been a long time since I'd had a friend to talk to. Our gazes caught and held, and I saw those brown eyes or even sympathy . . . just understanding.

Honestly, I never thought I'd solace in a ghost's touch and my throat grew tight as she continued to watch me.

I see ghosts.

I shook my head. "No. A year ago—when I woke up from the wreck, that's when I saw my first ghost.

Oh, and by the way, I saw you earlier at the house. "I admitted, wanting to return to less depressing topic.

She grinned, exposing deep dimples I hadn't notice before. How sad she had died so young. What a waste. "You did not let on that you could see me".

Josh wiggled his brows. "That was my intention. Then again, I didn't expect you to follow me to the bedroom.

"I was curious about you and your wife. The house had been empty for ten years.

CHAPTER 50

A Dark place

She laughed—a deep, rumbling sound that sent a spike of pleasure through me.

"I shall see you soon, Josh said, fading faster by the second.

"I refrained from looking over my shoulder one more time to see If Connie was still there.

I woke at ten thirty to the sound of Connie.

"IT's about time I got up, Connie.

She so didn't say anything at that moment.

I was hungry though, and my stomach chose that moment to growl.

Connie smiled. "I tell you what—you need to be careful of the dark shadow.

"I will.

"Usually sections of the house are open for unwanted visitors.

I had no intention of waiting to see the ghosts.

I left the house and crossed the road, passing by the garage that was packed and the shed where a few shadows sat out on a bench, staring at me.

On every street corner, they were there staring at me, and I couldn't get away.

I walked over to the cemetery, saw her name.

I looked down at the stone near the river, remembering her face.

I could end up in a mental hospital if I told someone that I see and talk to the dead.

I will end up in the looney bin.

Later that night, I heard some dogs growling and people were screaming for help. No one was to be found, so I closed the door, and I sat quietly in the corner to make sure no one had seen me. The wind was blowing and the lights went out, and I was really scared that I couldn't move.

About one hour later, I thought I heard someone knocking at the door, but I was afraid to open the door.

So I kept quiet and hope that they were be leaving, so I just kept quiet and hope that they were leaving.

I have never seen that person before. The wind blows out and it was gone.

At this point, I really didn't know what would happen next.

I closed my eyes and I prayed to God it would be gone.

I looked around and it seemed to be fine. So I went to check if the phone was working, but it was dead, and now.

I didn't know what to do.

Once again I looked out of my room and it seemed to be normal.

So I thought to myself, probably I should leave the house.

So I grabbed my car key, and I was about to step out, but I thought, no I am staying in. Then I saw his face, and I hurried to close the door. I also put a chair against the door to keep it shut.

Then I went to the table. I took a flashlight and I had to find my candles for light.

I was worried that the flashlight would run out of batteries and died.

The winds would hit the windows, but I kept on seeing his face.

For about one hour I sat on the bed, and read a book.

Then the phone rang, and I almost fell off the bed onto the floor. I was surprised that the phone was working at that time. I picked up the phone, but I didn't hear anyone there.

"I said hello, but no one answered. So I hung up the phone, and then it rang again.

"Now I was undecided, should I answer the phone or not."

I was shaking all over and I was really scared at this moment.

But don't be afraid of me, I will not harm you." "Well, I never met a ghost before.

CHAPTER 51

Ghost within us

Josh walks out of the house, and Ghost was waiting for him.

I must leave this place, it was gone.

So Josh walked into the street and then he reached the house and walked inside.

Later that day, Josh decided to take a walk to the basement, and everything seemed very quiet and strange. I kept on walking until I got there, and I walked inside. I looked around and everything seemed ok.

So I walk down the stairs, but then I saw the dead body on the floor. At that moment I wanted to scream, but I felt like paralyzed and I couldn't move.

So I left the basement, and ran all the way upstairs and locked the basement door. But I felt that someone was following me at that time.

So I hid in the closet for hours.

I was hesitated to come out of the closet, but then I heard someone calling my name.

I looked out and it was Star.

At the second I opened the door, I looked at her very carefully and she seemed to be all right.

I didn't say come in and take a seat, but then I saw her clothes, and immediately closed the door and said, "Get out of here now! What wrong Josh? I don't want you here get out now. Fine I will leave.

But I have to tell you the reason that I came to see you, is to warn you not to stay in this house.

I don t want to hear from you anymore and go away, leave me alone.

"Well, be on your own, and see how far you will get.

No, no one can save you.

Because you are a ghost, I don't want you around.

"Stop talking about it, then Star just vanished in thin air and she was gone.

Meanwhile Josh was looking around the house, then he heard a creaks near the door. He thought to himself, that I must get the heck out of this house.

I don't want them to fine me.

So Josh packed up and left the house.

So Josh got his stuff into the car. Josh was backing up, and he looked both ways and he put on the radio and the radio was static.

Josh drove into the road toward the highway to the city, to get away from the ghosts.

Josh started to listen to what Connie was saying to him, you will never get way from here, do you hear what I am saying, Josh.

So Connie kept on following him and he saw her in his rear window.

About a minute later she was gone.

Then Josh stop the car and got out of the car and looked around and when back inside and drove away.

Once again, he heard Connie and saying you are in danger and you cannot escape your fate.

No, you are dead, Connie, I am alive.

About a minute later, someone was in back of him. Josh turned around, and then the ghost was standing next to him.

Then Josh got touch his neck and said, what happened to me?

One minute later, Josh woke up from a deep sleep, and he's was bedroom, of the house.

About half hour later, I saw Connie standing there and she was looking straight into my eyes. At that moment, I was about to open the door, and then I shut my eyes and close the door.

About two hours later, I heard someone was calling my name. I came out and Star said, well what did you do with Lee?

CHAPTER 52

Gable rising

What do you mean? I don't have Lee, you did Star, and I don't remember that's!

You are confuse and don't listen what I am saying, Josh.

So what wrong with you and I just left you about ten minute ago, and you look at me like I am a ghost.

Josh noted the urgency in Star's voice and he knew that she was near him.

"Poor Josh" Star said. Josh looked up at the gable rising over the bedroom door.

"This house was everything to him.

IT sometimes difficult to remain aloof to the emotions of my family members, Josh knew that, but you simply could get emotions get the best of Josh.

"Bullshit, said Josh, that's not what mean at all. The place is cursed and haunted.

Josh didn't question the superstition.

Josh stood there in the bedroom and stare at the walls.

Cracks radiated out from the hole like spider legs. Somehow after failed attempt, Josh got push down the stairs.

Josh managed to get up and stagger a few feet across the floor where he collapsed before the fireplace, beneath the inscription on the mantel that read: Mine, always mine, Love Star.

Josh shook his head and blinked back the tears; there were things that surpassed all understanding.

Josh noticed that the floors were in need resurfacing, which meant that soaked deeply into the floor.

He stood and looks around and saw the "shadows".

Josh knew to looks into the kitchen and so the ghost followed Josh into the kitchen and knocked him down on the kitchen floor.

Josh knew that he was not alone.

Josh paused, trembling lips and knew that they were attack him at that moment.

Later that night, as he lay on the floor in his house, watching was going on in the house.

Sounds provided some unexplainable psychic link his wife, almost as through Josh could bring Star back.

Two weeks Josh was getting more paranoid and crazy talking and seeing ghosts.

No one didn't believe Josh and they thought he needed medical health, and it was he needed was mental help.

Josh written in an unfamiliar scrawl, it was an emotional, barely coherent letter, in which Josh rambled on about a nighttime, about finding the bodies in his basement.

Josh had things gone so horribly wrong?

Although naturally right cleaning solution over the bloodstains on the floor.

Nothing normal finding a dead body in a home is something wrong.

The handprint on the wall spots from the lounger to the hearth, came up easily, and needed a little more work, but it too finally eradicated.

Josh was worried that he were be accuse of the murders.

"What are you talking?"

Josh voice was irritation.

Later that day, Josh saw Star one more time, and she was crying.

Josh wanted to touch with his hand, and his hand when through her body.

Well, at least it wasn't as noisy as it was twenty hours a day. The demon could have done with more quiet, but it was adequate enough that it could emerge without causing a stir.

IT wasn't that impressive a being, this demon.

CHAPTER 53

"Shadow of two Globes

That is what it is, STAR. And like it all this kin, this Star was just a big blob of shadows two globes of light for her eyes.

The only obvious sign of individuality among the Star are the color of their eyes is matter of choice. It has bright violet eyes because it liked the color violet.

Star is a typical of a girl liked Pink.

The blob of shadow bounced out from the wall, glad to be rid of the foul ghost out of my house.

Drawing attention was not on the top of my list. But Josh's seen to try to get rid of the demon in the house.

Josh shivered and trembled at the thought the danger of dealing with the demon.

What that smelled.

Not a lot of human, but a demon.

The demon stalked me I am the prey by the few lengths more before it pounced.

Suddenly, the human spun at her heels and threw something in the face of mine.

With a yell of agony, the demon reeled back, but the salt was already burning its skin.

When it landed on the floor, poisonous silver pierced its shadowy flesh and its body dispersed into trickles of smoke.

Josh stared coldly at the remains of Star, just vanished.

Come back, I need to see you again, don't leave me, Star.

"You sound a little disappointed, Josh,"

Josh heard Star soft voice and said, I hear you but I don't see you.

Josh stand and she was behind him and the room got cold with a chill, and cold breathe.

Josh could hear scurrying around. The cold night air become colder and his cell phone rang with old fashion ring, a warning.

These demons are rude and dangerous to be around them.

Globes of lights rose from the floor and surrounded Josh, illuminating his face made a serene by the warmth by the spell brought.

But where the light gave comfort to the humans, it burned the demon of the dark. They recoiled and hissed as Josh retreated. However, that he would be no escape tonight for Josh.

Tonight Josh might not survive it.

The globes flashed bright and burst into one big globe that expanded throughout the whole house and the outside.

The sonic boom that followed would spread even further spelling the end would be for Josh.

Josh suddenly felt drained after having cast such a spell, but he had managed to fight off the fatigue just enough to get away.

There is a large room traditional at the outskirt of the house, most of the activities occurs.

I should have realized that something was up when I bought the house so cheap.

One day I ended up falling down the stairs for no reason at all, and I think that I been pushed by a ghost.

I feeling desperate and needed help, so I hired Ghost Hunter to come to my house and they did the investigated but never been seen again.

Even if this was going to hurt me I had to stay in the house.

I still don't know what happen to Star, and Lee and Connie and paranormal investigate.

I am sensitive and I do see things like vision and seeing the dead.

CHAPTER 54

Between life and death

Josh had a pleasant smile on his face and lazy spark in his eyes.

I was still stuck with being attack any second by a ghost that wanted to kill me.

At this point I didn't know what to do?

Then I felt the wind and it was coming toward me and I saw that dark shadow, and I couldn't escape and then it just was about to drag me and somehow it didn't catch me.

I was relief but still not safe at this point. I was still in danger and fear of my life.

Plenty of dangerous ghostly mischief was played and always, there was the dark shadow intervening. Josh banished the ghosts, stopped this chaos, and protected of my life.

Josh decided to have a séance at his house and invited a few friends and a medium.

Josh and his friend came over and sat at the table and then the medium arrive and they when into the room, where the table was locate and then they put their hands together and the séance started.

Suddenly the table move up and then they saw shadows coming closer and one of the guest just vanished and she was gone, and the light flicker and the low humming began and it got louder and louder.

Then the footsteps came closer and closer and a big bang and boom behind the door, and then the door open and no one was there.

The lights were switched off, the single candle at the center of the circle table set in the center of the library the only light.

While the small group at the table tried not to hyperventilate, the medium made the calls, saying there is a little girl in a pink dress standing near the table.

There were usual chills and there was the scratching. Cries of agony and sob of pain and regret pierced his heart. There was a lot of suffering.

Josh had felt their cries of warning when he first set foot near the table.

He told the others but he ignored it.

Mostly because he knew that running away is useless, after what happened next the door slammed and they couldn't escape and they all were trapped inside the library.

The hauntings started, six people disappeared and were never heard again."

"I sensed a total of thirty ghosts, Josh said.

Any fear I had of living there came solely from her.

She'd show up in the middle of the night, beating the door, screaming at her to open.

That's night I'd been soaking in the tub and decided to try to communication with the ghost. At that time, I had a name for her. It wasn't her real name of course, but it seemed to suit my mental picture of her. So many years have passed I've forgotten it now.

I'd been in the tub at least a half hour when I had the strangest feeling I needed to get out and get dressed. I didn't budge to start with, but the feeling grew stronger and the water got cold, so I did exactly that. No sooner than I'd put clothes on, Star burst through the door, slammed it and locked both locks.

Her pale skin was whiter than I'd ever seen I'd ever seen it. She was absolutely petrified.

Josh said she going to kill me.

About that time, the entry door stairs slammed. From the bottom of stairs, Josh screamed,

Thump, thump, thump echoed up the stairwell as he made way to the door.

Josh, go to the bedroom and locked the door,"

"Locks won't keep her out".

The door rattled on its hinges with the force of the first impact, but the locked held.

I bent my knees in anticipation of her entry.

CHAPTER 55

Lost spirit

Another boom announced his second hit. IT seemed stronger than the one before. Once again the door rattled violently. The locks still held.

The third hit sounded as if he'd thrown her massive body against the paneled door.

Soon the sound of walking footsteps and yelling wafted through the door. Another slam followed by ghost knocking on the door, and the door open.

I moved into the narrow hallway to see what she was going to do next.

Between Josh and the ghost, Josh was scared.

Just the over active imaginations of seeing Connie, Star, Lee that all coincidence.

To this day, I still love the smell of rose perfume.

However, one night it wasn't terribly of seeing ghost standing next to me.

No, it's not you, I-I just can't go home, this is my home.

Josh took a deep breath and grabbing my hand, pulled me into the living room.

Josh said my house is haunted.

I sleep alone in the house something whispers my name in my ear and wakes me up.

After my experience with the ghost: it would have been hypocritical for me not to.

I know it haunted and I'd already had an experience with ghosts, so no big deal, but they sometime attack me.

I did not feel uncomfortable, but I stayed and I didn't listen to Star and I had loss her. I will never see her again, in human form.

I tried a few times, but found continuously checking on her to make sure she was still breathing. Probably normal behavior for Star, but then again, I wasn't the 'freaking out' kind of person.

The first few times it happened, laughed about it. Maybe hallucinations or something, like seeing a ghost?

Twenty-one days after we moved in, the scary stuff began. Josh, my wife Star and her friend came over for sleep over.

Josh had left to go hiking with friends, leaving me and Lee home.

Lee sat on my lap was we practiced the alphabet.

All the sudden, Lee glanced over my shoulder toward the door. Star stopped talking and her face went white.

Star looked terrified. I turned to see what was looking at, and the face of a lady peered through the window in the back room.

Her shaggy, brown hair hung limply around her round face.

The dark circles under her eyes could have been cuts. Her face unblinking, she stared at me. Then she was gone. " Poof" Nothing.

Her face appeared in my dining room window.

I was stunned and I couldn't move.

She disappeared again, and my body went into overdrive.

Standing in the middle of the room gave me a clear view of the living room and front door.

She looked right at me.

No expression on her face whatsoever. No fear, no recognition that I was about to hide and she was gone.

No way!

You tell me to get someone around back and when they knock on my door, I ran and hid in the closet.

"No I haven't lived here long."

The ghost think you saw would have been here had been murder in the house.

There no footprints and a lot sound of heavy footstep coming closer to us.

CHAPTER 56

Ghost girl

Except for the woman in the window, most of the activities seemed playful and childlike. At times I nearly convinced myself that it must be the ghost of youngster playing pranks. Other times, it was difficult to live in that delusion.

The overwhelming feeling of dread and fear that emanated from the bedroom could be completely, debilitating.

The feeling weren't subtle and came on quickly. I could walk by the bedroom door 20 times and feel nothing.

My heart racing would thud against my chest so hard it was actually in pain.

IT only lasted a few seconds, but that was long enough to scare the crap out of me.

By then, the ghost had added something new to her bag of tricks.

No matter which room I was in, I would see this white mist in my peripheral vision.

As soon as I'd realize it was there, I'd turn to look and it would be gone. I got smart after a while. I stopped looking head on and would watch it from the corner of my eye. The mist itself was nearly transparent.

Almost like a spheres shaped cloud of smoke. It hovered about a foot from my bed.

Now, I was feeling a faint feeling and Star just collapsed to the floor. About half hour later, Star was surrounded by the ghosts.

All the ghosts were smiling at Star. Follow us, Star.

So Star follows them to the basement and then the ghost girl's appear to Star.

But now Star was so quiet, and she showed Star the door and said "step inside" and I wants to show you something.

I believe that I should go back to upstairs, but I still follow the ghost girl into the some space in the basement and then it close behind me shut tight.

Why am I here? You will see in a second.

I don't understand what you are saying, very well.

Ghost came into the room, and girl ghost was standing in the mist.

Then ghost girl approaches toward Star.

"Don't do it."

What is Ghost girl saying, don't do it?

I really cannot say, but you should leave now, Star.

No, not without Lee!

I cannot let them go because my son's belong with me.

No!

You must come with me, said the ghost girl.

"You are ghost?

Yes I am comes with me and see Lee, your son.

"No, I am not going, bring Lee to me, said Star.

"IT is time to go back to upstairs, and you must follow me.

Don't you understand what I am saying?

Star calls out for Lee and no answer and not a sound.

Then I saw the little girl ghost dressed in pink dress and white shoes.

Star smiled at the little girl and she vanished in thin air.

"I want to show you something, Star, and the ghost girl said follow me.

"Where are you taking me?

Are we going to be long? I must show you where Lee is.

What? I don't understand, what you are saying.

Well I don't know what I will do with you, you are confusing me.

You are in danger said the ghost girl to Star, and I am sorry to bring you here.

CHAPTER 57

Cobwebs

So where is Lee? I don't know what. I didn't see him for hours; he must left the basement and I don't know where he is.

I need to find him.

"I can be alone without my son, and we are a family.

Star saw Lee for a brief moment and then Star didn't see him again.

Why are you leaving, Lee. I am your mother, do you hear what I am saying Lee.

Then the door open and Star steps inside the small space, and then the door shut behind her.

A little while Star was on the floor, and Lee stood and waited to listens what Star was going to says too him.

Then she looks in the mirror and saw her reflection and then saw Lee.

I have two marks on my arms. What have you done to me?

Later that night, she started to feel that she was not alive, anymore.

Two hour later, Star walks back to the upstairs and walks into the kitchen and everything seem to be different with cobwebs.

Star woke up and had a bad dream, and she said, I must find a way to get rid of the ghosts."

Star couldn't stop thinking about the bad dream that she had and was it real or was dreaming.

About five minute later, Star's was lays on her bed next to Josh and she saw a mist through the window, and saw his face.

Star was sitting on the couch and looking out of the window, and she thought she seen a ghost walking by her home.

Now she was wondering, what was going on in the house?

Star was thinking, how many ghosts they have in the house.

Meanwhile back in house where paranormal activity occurs went Star was alone.

Star got up and went to the kitchen to make dinner, and went she started she heard crackling sounds coming from the living room.

Then the dog started to bark at the door and Star peek out and no one was there.

About twenty minutes later, Star heard a lot of tapping near the house and she look out and no one was there.

Then Star saw her old friend who was dead, and she couldn't believe her eyes, what she was seeing.

So Star decided to calls Josh and telling him what was going on in the house.

But Josh said that he was busy and cannot talks with right now, and would see her later.

After talking with Josh, she hung up the phone and was too terrified to be alone in the house, and left the house.

Then Star said, well I have to go now, so I just lock up the house and went to the car and drove away.

Star thought to I did sees ghosts in my house and now they are following me.

One ghost that I seen was his eyes had a sparkled and kept staring at me.

The other ghost's that I seen would more creeping than this one and I cannot imagine what I need to do?

"I have gut feeling that this is not the end of the ghosts and haunting, I am fear they will hunted me and attack too.

My family will be in danger and I don't know what to do?

I will find a way to get rid of the ghosts and take my home back.

I am not giving up, the home that I love and I am not going to move.

"We have no place to stay.

I drove through the woods and then I stop the car and got out for a moment.

CHAPTER 58

Shadowy figure

About five minutes later, the phone rang, but I missed the call.

Later that night I got back home, and drove into the driveway and for a moment, I thought that I seen a shadowy figure standing near my front door.

Soon had I steps out of the car, I felt for a moment that the ghost would attack me instantly.

Suddenly, ghost's touched me and pushed me to the ground and I was laying there.

About a minute I got up and ran inside and now I know that I am being hunting by the ghost.

Ghost came up and said, I want you so badly.

Star started to run and run. Then she ran into Josh's arms.

Josh's asked what wrong?"

You are talking about the ghosts?

All of them they are in our home and they have our son, Lee.

I have heard them and that why I left the house.

Josh was walking around the house and suddenly Josh heard the low humming sound from the basement.

So Josh went to the basement to check it out and Star said please don't go you will gets hurt and Josh said I will be fine and don't worry about it.

Josh went downstairs and then the door shut and he was screaming and said get me out of here now.

About one minute, he saw a dead body of a man.

I cannot be here.

Went you came back with bruises and cuts and scratches and Star said what happened to you?

I believe that I got attack by a ghost. That what happened, Star.

Then he got closer to Star and said that we need to leave this house now.

Star said no, I am not leaving and I am staying.

About one minute later, they both heard a knock at the door and Josh was afraid to looked, they both looked and no one was there.

Then they heard rattled sound and then pots and pans were flying around in the kitchen and there was a white mist and shadowy figure standing near the door.

"Well I have a question to ask, why do we have ghosts in our home?

I don't know how to answered that's question.

Do see you see the mist? Yes I do.

I see the white most in my peripheral vision. As soon I'd realize it was there, I'd turn to look and it would be gone.

I got smart after a while. I stopped looking head on and watch it from the corner of while. I stopped looking head on and would watch it from the corner of my eye. The mist itself was nearly transparent. Almost like a sphere shaped cloud of smoke, it hovered about a foot from the floor. As long as I didn't look at it directly, it would stay for several minutes at a time.

IT's not that she didn't believe me, he saw the mist too. She was there when things disappeared. She just didn't believe there was anything to be afraid of.

And if it weren't for that occasional heart pounding fear, I'd have agreed with her.

She didn't say a word but all the color drained from her face.

I spun around to see what she was looking at. A short shadow shaped like a woman, paced along the bedroom. I gasped and the shadow stopped and turned to face me. It looked as if it were staring right at me. Within seconds it took off and went down the wall disappearing into the living room.

This house is haunted!

"Did you see that?"

She finally asked.

"I told you."

"I know. But did you see that?"

She shook her head and pulled Josh to a standing position.

"Don't get freaked out. It's just a ghost. They can't hurt us."

Yours wrong they can hurt us and yours very wrong about that.

No, I am not.

IT was a dark and stormy night.

I jest, but it was very horrifying experience. Even now, it freaks me out to think about it. Worse, fear that most folks believe in ghosts and some are skeptic.

Star said about one week ago I saw the shadow and things escalated.

Josh's rhythmic snoring irritated me at first, but finally lulled me to sleep. I don't know what woke me up. One minute I sound asleep, and the next sitting straight up in my bed. I listened intently for noise or some sign of what was wrong.

Something had to be wrong. I could feel the wrongness of the situation deep within me. My heart raced so fast and hard that made it difficult to hear much of anything.

I took a few deep breaths, closed my eyes, and laid back down. Seconds turned into minutes as I waited for my thudding heart to still.

Instead of diminishing the feeling of wrongness amplified. Fear grew and blossomed into full blown terror as I listened to the quiet house.

"NOTHING"

Not one sound that wasn't completely ordinary and easily explained.

The refrigerator fan kicked on, making me jump.

The dark feeling would not go away.

I don't know how long I laid there before I noticed that I was clenching my eyes shut.

CHAPTER 59

Bad feeling

You can image how ridiculous I felt. I pulled up the blanket up over my head out to grab me.

Without second thought, I pulled up the blanket over my head and opened my eyes.

I pushed the blanket away and surveyed the door room.

The heavy blinds over the window let in just enough light to leave dark shadows in the corner of the room. The rocking chair, piled high with towels.

I had yet to fold and put away in the morning.

Sighing, I placed my hands behind my head, and contemplated my insanity.

I must be nuts, right?

I mean who act like that? Sheesh!

I watched the ceiling fan go round and round, hoping that at some point it would hypnotize me and put me to sleep. Above the fan the ceiling itself was so black I could only see the outside edges.

I rubbed my eyes as darkness seemed to grow the than the fan. IT stretched and elongated until it was oval shaped. My breathing became labored. And as badly as I wanted to close my eyes, they would not even allow me to blink.

Star was frozen.

I tried to move.

I tried to reach out and grab Josh.

With every ounce of strength I had, I had, I tried to put my hand on Josh shoulder and shake him. My body refused to obey the mind's commands.

The darkness retreated slowly, and once again the shadow above the bed was the size and shape it should been.

Tears streamed down my face, and not wanting to wake up Josh, I choked back sobs.

I couldn't speak. All I could do was curl up in Josh arms and cry, and that's what I did.

The next morning, I told Josh what had happened and that we had to move.

Josh, of course, told me I was crazy. "IT must have been a nightmare.

Maybe a night of terror or something, I cannot explain it.

Star knew it wasn't something like that.

Star knew it wasn't anything like that!

I'd make my mind up and regardless of whether Josh was willing or not, I was moving. There was no way I would keep Lee in that house for any longer than necessary.

I have calls Josh.

I hadn't told him about the new place or moving, no matter what he'd said—I knew wherever we were.

(Now I know you're going think I'm crazy, but I SWEAR this is true)

"Have you lost your mind? We can't afford to move again!" Josh exclaimed.

Josh let out an exasperated breath and didn't say another word.

Star can't live here.

Something's very wrong with this place.

IT's not safe for Lee.

If it can do what it did last night, it will harm us all.

I'd had enough experiences with ghosts to notice a house was haunted before we moved in. Honestly, I had a 'feeling' something was haunted before we moved in. However, it wasn't a bad feeling. In fact, it reminded me tremendously of my protector.

Star noticed things right away. Our 'friends' weren't even remotely shy.

A strange scraping noise, like wood rubbing together, floated up the stairs.

Josh and Star sat up in bed.

We traded glances and headed for the stairs. Before I reached the stairs, I heard the door and headed for the stairs, I heard the door to the bedroom.

I stayed close him.

Of course there was no one there.

I went outside and wandered around the exterior of the house for a bit.

I locked the door, laughed about the strangeness of it, and went inside.

Star and went back to bed.

The next morning, Star awoke and headed down to make breakfast.

As soon Josh entered the kitchen, I stopped short. Once again, the back door stood wide open, and suddenly the door shut tight.

Feeling foolish, but still certain something out of the ordinary had occurred; I saw the dark figure standing against the wall.

Once again I heard the scraping noise again.

The footsteps came right up to our door and just stopped.

I just had this feeling . . . '

Josh eyes rolled and Josh shook his head. "Don't start that crap again. Josh's are not moving.'

Laughing, I answered, OF course we're not moving. Don't be ridiculous.

There's nothing wrong with this house.

As the days passed' the nightly sliding of the pocket doors and the footsteps on the continued. Occasionally the back door would be open in the night.

I was slightly concerned, but they weren't telling me' ghost' stories, so I let it go.

A loud scream followed by, Star, Star, Star!' jolted me from deep sleep.

I recognized Connie's voice instantly and headed to room. As soon as the light was switched on, she bolted out of bed and wrapped her arms around me.

Tears poured from Connie from her eyes as she sputtered between sobs.

CHAPTER 60

Creeps me out

Star had been asleep, but a strange noise woke her.

Her eyes snapped open and across the room from her in the chair, young woman sat watching a small girl was playing with a doll.

Her description of both the woman and the girl were extremely vivid.

She said the girl was about Susan's size youngest, and wore pink dress with white socks and white shoes.

The woman wore her hair in a ponytail and had long old timey dress on.

At first she was just shocked, but when the woman looked away from the girl to glare at her, it terrified me.

Star opened her mouth to scream for help.

Lady bent forward and raised her finger to her lips.

At that point I screamed my head off, and Josh was running in.

It wasn't long after that I saw my first apparition in my house.

My experience was complexly different, and the way it came about coupled with the small event from earlier that day, leads me to believe the ghost I saw had nothing to do with the house per se.

I believe that particular ghost was attached to thing instead of a place.

I'd decided to do some digging around. There were two attics in the house. One was a walk in attached to my living room, and the other on could entered through a large door in the downstairs near the kitchen. Both were absolutely full.

Being the nosey person I was, I decided to rummage around and see what sort of trinket had been left behind from owners.

I entered the attic attached to my living room.

Neatly stacked boxes covered the floor making difficult to maneuver.

Star started with the boxes closet to the door and worked back. Most were filled with junk. Those went to the left out to the recycle bin barrel.

About the midway through the small room, I'd just moved a stack of boxes and notice the front of larger picture. I turned it around and let out a gasp.

About a minute later a little girl stared back at me with the saddest hazy eyes I'd ever seen. She had long brown ponytail and dressed in s knee length brown winter coat that matched her eye color exactly.

Her tiny pink lips were pulled up in a pout. IT was adorable and I loved it. IT was easy to see it was hand painted and canvas looked old, but the frame was gold plastic with large ornate scrolling prevalent in the 1970's. IT didn't seem to fit with the look or age of the painting, said Star.

I took it downstairs and I got to work on it right away. After removing the canvas from the frame, I used the softest cloth I could find out and meticulously ran it over every inch of the painting. It took at two hour work on the frame.

After Star dusting and scrubbing, the plastic frame still looked cheap gold plastic.

That would not do for this beautiful piece of art.

Star sanded it a bit and carefully spray painted it black.

After the paint dried and the two pieces had been fitted back together, Star hung it on the wall in the living room.

Star was terribly proud of how well it turned out.

The now black frame looked like old wrought iron. Star couldn't wait to do some research and find out how old the painting really was.

Unfortunately, Josh wasn't nearly as thrilled with my find.

Josh said it creep me out, Josh said.

Star insisted the painting in the living room would stay on the wall.

That night, after the usually complaints about not wanting to sleep upstairs, I finally fell asleep.

Sometime in the middle of night I felt a finger poking my shoulder. I was so tired I didn't even bother to open my eyes. Josh's asked what wrong?"

Josh asked what wrong, Star"

Recognizing the little girl voice, yet still unable to force my eyes open, I repeated, "what wrong Josh?"

The poking began again. Five distinct pokes to my shoulder.

Each punctuated, "Star"!

My little visitor didn't bother me again that night, but somehow—and I wonder now if it wasn't the care of her painting that brought it on—she'd attached to me. From the point on, I saw her nearly every day. Not full on, like the first time. Here and there I'd catch a glimpse of brown streak across my peripheral vision.

Sometimes, when the house was completely empty, I'd hear softy call out, "Star?" Over the two years lived there, I'd taken to speaking to her outright.

At times I'd catch a glimpse out of my corner of my eye and soon after hear a soft of laughter as if as if she were playing hide and seek.

Sometimes I'd play along and other times I'd say, "Not right now, said Star.

I'm busy. Wait until I am home alone in the house.

Of course it all sounds rather crazy now, and Josh said who are you talking too?

No, one Josh, okay.

I closed my eyes and it was silent grew wider. I felt that I was not alone someone was in the room with me.

That's day numerous little things that happened in the house.

Disembodied whispers, and the sounds of evil laughter, and scampering feet, the heavier footsteps on the stair, and doors that opened and closed of their own accord, it got worst each day I stayed alone in the house.

I stayed in the house and Josh refuse to move and things got really bad and horrible, and I think it was going to kills us.

But I did mention that to Josh and he was a skeptic.

CHAPTER 61

Eerie screams

One day I was sitting in the living room and I heard a loud screams and I looked out and there was no one there.

I can see anything but the mist in the backyard and it was coming toward the back door.

"Who's out there?"

Who are you and what do you want from, me, you have taken Star and Lee from me and you have leaves me alone.

Josh noticed the male ghost was holding him and wanted to drag him and Josh just was not going to let him take him.

Now Josh had to save himself from the poltergeist, in his house. But the poltergeist was getting stronger and it had the power to get rid of Josh.

I don't know what happened next but I didn't see it again.

The moment I fight with it and it just disappears and it was gone.

Josh felt a trembling in his knees that he knew was not arthritis and down. "Stuck, ghost said in a small voice, "I will be back?"

Josh could even imagine such things? GHOSTS"

Josh stood up. I should have believes Star and she were not be dead, I should have believe her and now it is too late.

If I only hear her voice one more times.

Star come visit me, I need you so much.

But Josh was still skeptic but he just thought it was a bad dream, but the house was getting more noise and ominous sound and eerie coming closer to Josh.

Josh remembered a similar look into her eyes when she when she no longer here

He didn't know to deal with his grief, and it was hard and unyielding as stone.

Josh had a lot of obstacle and didn't know how to get back and just a lot of sadness, in his life. Every night Josh felt that he was being watched and someone was behind him.

When he turned around Ghost was standing in the room.

Josh lowered himself into the bed by the windows every joint in his body suddenly on fire. He sighed and looked at her, still standing before him, and he noticed that she was partial once again. He forced his eyes up to her face, and she was gone.

I know it was it hasn't been easy, but I cannot live without you.

"I thought about you often after you first visited. I miss you, Star.

Star sat in the chair beside Josh and gently took his hand, her touch warm and light, but he was upset that he couldn't feel her.

Star nodded her head and said I need to go now, and Josh said stayed with me.

No, I can't I need to go now. And she was gone.

Josh had tears in his eyes and how much he missed her and loved her.

The house just wasn't the same without you, and Lee?"

He reached out and grasped out to reach her but she was not in the room anymore.

Without her, here was like an empty house.

But the whispering in Living room and then the whole house like echo everywhere.

The slightest imperceptible sound could wake me in the middle of the night.

The rustling of tree branches like sandpaper being rubbed together, slight of whistling sound the wind made right before the storm, a murmur in the bedroom, and I could hear her all the time.

I looked I saw her standing near the bed and I was amazing that Star came to see to visit me, but she was not alone, but the dark force was also in the room.

Josh couldn't believe what he is seeing, but it just lasted for a minute.

Then like a wind came through and it both were gone.

I got up I saw something black just passing me through my body and I know it was not human.

I had a hard time believing I hadn't heard something abnormal, and so I decided again to spend the night at the hotel.

CHAPTER 62

Past Haunting

I can remember it all like happened yesterday, I remember things before they when too far. After I'd done it all, I was the same. There was something in the house, and I cannot explained it still haunt me.

I lost Star, I will not be the same again without Star I am alone.

To this day, I still smell her perfume of roses and I see her in that blue dress and those high heels.

The darkness of my home sneaking out into the night the longing to strike into something dangerous, that strike me dead if I don't leave this house, and I won't be seen again.

The chill of the ghosts that are being more aggressive, they will attack me and I will be killed and there will be no trace of me in this house.

Each night I do get a warning but I think I can beat them, I might be delusion.

I refuse to leave my home. I need to found Star and Lee.

Josh nightmares are getting worst each day, after the assembly but all will be forgotten, with the event of this house, one thing to another.

IT was phenomenon that I been chase by a ghost, not at first went we first move in but several month when by and started with humming and low thudding in the house and I refuse to listen to Star, and she wanted to move out and I said no.

At that time I was a skeptic but now I do believe in ghost.

I'd thought the encounter had been strange, and frightfully similar to the stories.

One day the front door opened, and it appear and in front of me and then it was gone.

I decided to takes pictures and then I saw some creep pictures that I development and I saw some shadows in the pictures.

I couldn't believe what I was seeing.

What do you wants from me?

I heard a roar—I couldn't make out the words, but the tone was clear—ghost.

There was scuffing, then ghost again in the background.

I got pushed.

I was stalked by a ghost, and I heard ghost conversations and I yelled out said leave me alone.

They are coming?

Josh saw a face of ghost and said no, leave me alone.

Sometimes it was just bad night, and I could do nothing to do and I just had the lights on and I felt safer.

I could do nothing to get them out of my house.

Something came into my imagination as frequent torture, and it got worst take my word.

Sometimes when it was night, and dark, I would be tremble and tremendous imagination: I imagined with clarity of senses and full belief, that a ghost was stalking me. Somehow, I couldn't tell how it was about to get me in a hurried.

IT had been watching from the other room, and then suddenly it was behind me.

I started to have panic attack, I might die—forget that I knew intellectually that it taunt me daily.

His mouth worked soundlessly for a moment, and he blinked. I . . . I just had a bad dream."

The light snapped on, flooding the room with a warm light, and Star's sleep-addled face slid from the cover as she was alive.

Josh yelled and slid away, falling out of bed onto the floor. Josh hand scrambled for the switch on his bedside lamp, and he heard the thing shift in bed.

The sheets were cool, and he shivered and tried to calm his mind.

CHAPTER 63

High-pitched shriek

His mind skipped and tried to grab hold amidst the pin wheeling emotions.

Josh shook his head. I have to get out of here," Josh said, and backward toward the blackened window that led to the roof of the garage.

"I have to-"

Ghost's high pitched shriek cut his word off. Josh jumped to his feet and tried to turn, but hunched over the pain and gave scared.

Its eyes were rolled up to the whites it was horrible to look at.

Josh realized his mouth was so dry he couldn't have said anything that night.

The pounding stopped and silence invaded the room. Josh swallowed and turned his eyes back to the door. Josh looked up and his hand motionless on the back of him.

An incessant pounding throbbed against the door, like a ghosts hitting it all at once, that wouldn't let up.

Ghost told me he'd kill me.

"Ghost came back."

Josh felt the doorknob beneath his palm begin to turn. Josh spun gripped it with both hands, his eyes registering that was still locked.

"Let me go, Josh said.

"The smell of death in the air"

"OH no, oh, no, oh, no, Josh moaned. Ghost stepped toward that moment and Josh though he's be a dead.

Josh strained forward toward the smaller flight of stairs to the right and grabbed the handle to his bedroom.

With the grunt Josh shoved the door inward and flung into the ghost.

He hit the light, and slamming it behind him once when he was inside.

The voice came from the bedroom, and Josh stopped in mid-step, fear punching him full in the chest. A tall shadow stood in the bedroom untouched by the light that tried to push him downstairs.

Josh sometime would hear walk into the room and see chair moving very gently, as if someone just left.

Once in a while one could have sworn one had just heard a voice in the next room.

On one occasion, a "female figure in white" walked through the bedroom where I sleep.

Were the spirits rising with the night approach the night? Did I sense something in the room right now?

Josh looked into the empty room. Josh saw nothing. Yet the feeling on the back of his neck remained.

Josh whispered to himself, "NO, one's not going to hurt me"

I reached the door to bedroom, the area that was pitched black.

I felt a prickly feeling at the base of my neck.

Josh also suffered from a sense of intrusion, as I had entered an area where many peoples had stopping talking and I holding silent.

I hesitated to go down staircase.

Ghosts prowled through the kitchen and opening cabinet doors.

Upstairs was a different story.

I had avoided to section of house in which the ghost had first been disturbed.

I reached the closet door and yanked it open, expecting the worst.

A few wire hangers hung undisturbed, swaying slightly from the vibration of the door.

I turned relieved, retraced my steps and walked back upstairs also I looked relieved at that moment.

Josh found the front door open.

CHAPTER 64

Whispered

Then an inner voice flirted with me again," Can't I see you?"

I blew out a long breath. I knew that I was psyching at that point. I knew it couldn't stop it.

Should I walk away from that closet?

The internal voice I asking myself all the questions what happen today?

The premonition was very strong before now.

Josh drew another breath and held it. I felt the sweat starting to run off me.

I pushed the door open.

Josh lowered his eyes, gathered his courage, and looked up searching quickly through the empty room as he stepped into it.

"Nothing, nothing at all an empty room's like the rest of the house?

Josh eyes settled upon a room. That door, too, partial open. And it was at the perfect angle so Josh couldn't see into it.

Josh courage faltered.

The second floor was more ominous. Josh's walking in the living room below.

I turned and walked down the hallway toward Lee room end of the second floor. "The area where the ghosts had appear the first day that we move into the house"

I wondered what horrible thing might lurk on the other side.

Josh drew a breath.

I reached the halfway point. Josh paused for a second then slowly climbed to stairs. Again, I expected some sudden spiritual manifestation as I took step by step.

I did feel something or someone at that point.

Then I peered upstairs again, half expecting some nightmarish devilish vision to charge down the stairs toward the ghost.

I saw the ghost. She came down the steps right over there.

I left the den and followed me into the corridor that led into an open dining room with a gorgeous old hearth.

I'd just like to be out of this situation. So would be haunted by those ghosts.

Josh I saw ghost.

And as far as I know, ghost continued, jingled the knob and turned it.

This ghost was right inside the house standing right next to me.

Watching me, and waiting for me.

But I was not going upstairs.

The door gave way easily and came wide open with a big silent yawn.

The two ghosts stepped inside, with the obvious apprehension.

I left the front door and walked into the den on the east side of the first floor.

The room was clean full with furniture and TV and bright.

Apparitions are part of an electrical process that we don't yet understand in terms of science.

I'd never seen before.

Two ghosts stood at the front door.

A cloud passed across the sun and they were abruptly in a shadow.

I didn't just walk away from this place and not seeing ghosts.

Josh locked the back door and when to his car and drove away from the house.

I got to the stop and looked back and didn't go back to the house again.

Josh just wanted to forget what happened in that house and losing Star and Lee, and never seen them again.

CHAPTER 65

Bad timing

One later afternoon, June and Robert drove into Windsor Connecticut, and they saw the house and June stop her car and said to Robert I like this place.

So June and Robert her standing outside of that house, and June said I would like to go inside, Robert said, I don't think so.

"Robert you sound like a scary cat"

June walk inside and Robert follow her inside and the door closing behind them.

Now June began to sense something is wrong in the house and June said let leave now.

She moved to the door and it won't open. Now we have a problem.

Don't tell me that we are trapped in this creepy house? I won't! What?"

He shrugged again.

I can't control that.

Robert was silent. He was terrified being in that house.

June said don't worried I will get us out of here, soon.

Robert blew out a long breath.

"Honestly I can't.

A churning head pounding brain chilling burst of fire forms and flies out of the body bringing the soul with it, hanging on behind like a shadow.

IT's like having your feeling ripped out from you a thousand times worse than emotions you felt as a human, a squashing of time and sorrow into your new existence and form.

Imagine, if we don't make out alive from here. What are you saying, June.

I should tell you about when I become a ghost sometime soon, what are you saying that is?

It's probably the best thing I ever did.

So you are talking about ghosts? Yes I am.

That's the thing about ghosts.

But always and often too soon we have to leave and yes I agree, June.

Yes, you've guessed it, the human stress and dismay at waking into a haunted house and then something happened and you end up dead and you become a ghost.

Perhaps we should leave, and Robert goes close to the door and unable to open it's, and now Robert is freaking out and I want to get the hell out now.

I, can feel the tiniest shiver down my back and the ghost is behind me.

For a brief moment we have a chance to escape from this house.

"After an hour and they still were in the house and June and Robert, had no ways out".

It's was been sucks on in times of crisis; it got no exude any emotions.

Dragging it down darkness, and end up being here forever that sucks.

No worrying about you leaving me behind, Robert you are giving up.

No I am not, but the door won't open don't you get it June, why did bring us here?

I don't know but I heard about this place and I was curious about this place and I just wanted to take a peek.

You and I might end both us being ghosts here.

June pushed the door and it would not move and Robert tried to help.

"I know what you asked me," Robert parried. "And you also know what I answered."

"I did."

CHAPTER 66

Paranormal Activities

Josh returns to the house, after two years.

I heard something else join the sounds of footsteps coming toward me.

He stopped and stared at the end of the hall, listening carefully. At first he could only hear the sound of his heart thumping in his chest and thought that might losing his mind, but then he heard it again.

Something was making its way toward me from the other side of the corridor.

Josh tried to tell himself that is was someone simply exiting the bathroom and making it their way back to me, and I listened the less I believed myself.

I next inclination was to turn around and run back out of the door.

Josh was wrong and really had been only inside a few minutes ago.

The sound grew louder and louder to Josh and found himself desperately wishing he had never entered the house at all.

Only Josh wasn't quite convinced it was water. IT's sounded mores dense than that to him.

As he stood there, frozen with of sick anticipation, he saw what it was.

Blood crept across the walls from around the corner like some kind of oozing overflow. Then he heard the footsteps again and this time they sounded nothing like that of his own. It sounded as if something light was being dragged across the floor.

With each footstep he noticed ripples running in the pool of blood, which had now reached the block wall and was beginning to push toward him.

From around the corner a moan echoed, sending chill through his entire body.

The moan seemed to die off a second and then another, more powerful one, followed.

Something appeared at the corner of hall, moving slowly and unsure at first. It was wearing a blue jean and a white tee shirt.

Its eyes rolled slowly around to view the rest of the hall and suddenly locked on Josh. As ghosts widened, a sort of primordial excitement coursing through ghost, and the ghost's arms—or what was left of them—reached out of Josh.

Josh tired again to move his legs and this time, much to his surprise, found himself backing away from the ghost and to the entrance of the door.

The ghost began to move toward him, its arms still stretched out, only this time when it moved it picked up speed. Josh turned around and immediately headed for the front doors, running as fast as he could. Josh could hear the ghost was heaving breathing, behind Josh.

Josh scream for help and something more terrifying than anything could ever have imagined happened. Josh found himself surrounded by more ghosts, their hideous faces watching Josh.

Ghosts reached out for Josh, and as they did Josh fell hard on the ground.

The next morning Josh was still screaming when Josh woke up that morning.

Josh sat straight up his sleep, grasping for air and soaked in sweat. Josh looked around and he knew that he was not alone.

Josh saw that everything was still as it had been before his very own vivid nightmare.

He swallowed hard, soothing his dry and irritated throat, and ran.

He wished he could forget what happened that night.

Looking back over all of that he could see how insignificant that really was, but still didn't change his mind what he saw last night.

He didn't know how he really felt about ghost other than if was real.

He shook off his ghosts thoughts for a moment, almost tripping over a crack of the patio.

He had never see ghost quite so dark before.

Just then Josh dream came back to him. The sounds the ghosts had made and the blood slowly drifting toward Josh.

Josh shrived before descending down a hills.

CHAPTER 67

Paranormal Activities 2

Josh had never had dream that had seemed so real before. Sure, he had dreamed of seeing Star and Lee going away.

But there was something about this dream that was different.

Usually Josh dreamt about places he had been recently, or had been concentrating on quite some time. This dream had place in a dark place that he doesn't want to see again.

Josh hadn't been that impressed with, what was going with his mind.

Thinking about it now, even almost wanted to cry.

Josh reminded of the scary stories that family told him about the haunted house and about ghosts.

He still remembered most of them to this day; there's was the one's day where the ghost, just so took his hand and pull it one night.

Josh did not forget about the hauntings that's he experience in the past and present.

He started ahead, trying not to notice the ghosts around him as they talked voices of echoed.

'Every once and while Josh looked down at saw the one partial ghost staring at him"

Then he's walk over to me and grabbed my hand and pulled me away and like trying to take me from this world.

At that moment I thought I would be a goner, but then the humming and thudding started and footstep got closer and closer to me.

The lights flicker on and off and then the motion stop, for a second.

Echoed throughout the house and it was no escape and then the door shut tight and I was unable to open them.

Now I knew that I thought something terrible will happen to me.

But I didn't run and I thought I would be fine even though I had threatened and warning but I still stayed in the house.

Josh looked at wall and it was dripping of bloods everywhere.

That's sounds evil, but what exactly at that point I don't know.

I'd say keeping my mind focus and distancing from the ghosts that I was doing.

The moment ghost reached out to my hand and the air got colder and colder and I felt the cold breath, and the chill in the air. I know I was not alone and I didn't know what to do at this point.

But they were still with me and I was surrounded and I just stood there.

My experience was scary and terrified at the same time.

I felt sensed the mood changing in the house.

I knew obviously and the changes were not a good sign for me.

Josh could almost see them clearly has they were standing next to him.

But the pounding was getting loud and the tapping was coming from the kitchen and about two sets of footstep were coming toward me at one moment of time.

"IT just seems to me it would not end in a good ways.

Josh looked at them and they were creeps me out.

I heard more conversation, turning the attention my way, at that moment I just jump up.

Josh shrugged, turning back around and ghost were there standing by me.

"I can't believe, what happening right now too me.

They won't let me go.

The feeling is eerie and ominous and it really dark and spooky and I don't know if I will make it out alive.

I had heard stories about this place but I was a skeptic and now I am not.

"What I have seen you would not believe me, but I have seeing ghost wandering in the house and I had been touch"

The point after dark in this house you would get the willies and you wouldn't want to stay here at night.

"Unbelievably bright light emitting inside the house"

There was a slight haze hovering above the attic that night and the house.

The moon had shine one of the room of the house and within the last hour and although I saws shadows at that instant of time.

I reached over and grabbed Star hand, placing it in my hand.

Then I looked and it was not "STAR" but the poltergeist that wanted to take me to hell.

Poltergeist was not going to take me to hell.

At that's moment just disappear in thin air and I ran out of the kitchen.

IT had been a night I would never forget, so long has I live.

Josh stopped feeling something cold on his shoulder, Josh looked to his right and a damp smell hit him, instantly making him nauseous and gag.

He couldn't make out what on his shoulder but of corner of his eye could see something like a hand.

He tried to get to the hand and force it off the shoulder and it was gone in a second.

I began to scream, I had terror echoing down the spine of my back.

"Suddenly, the forced on his back by a large, rotting ghost"

The two ghosts let out unearthly moans, filled with fluid, as I struggled with ghosts.

Within minutes I silenced and saw their body lay lifeless on the ground.

The noise level inside was absolutely incredible.

I finally walk out of the kitchen into the living room, and sat for a while.

An enormous sound from the upstairs and I think it was from the attic.

I approached the stairs but then I change my mind.

At that moment once again I was surrounded by ghosts and I couldn't move.

Do you really want them to?

I caution you to remember . . . I went through many events and occurrences in this house.

If the last miraculous thing can be rationalized away, haven't I lost the mind of the unknown?

"A truthful accounting of a paranormal experience"

"I only know what's exactly happened in this house and it were been me.

Josh known for year and have no reason to believe that anything would like this.

Please keep in mind I am not the only one's seen ghosts.

I protection the identities of those involved, the names of people, town have been changed.

I made mistakes in my life.

I'd barely learn from colossal blunder buying this house, and losing loved one.

I had a hard time believing the truth and what Star was saying to me, and I should have listening.

But I was stubborn and I was a skeptic and now I am alone in this haunted house.

But not anymore, I seen it all and I don't know if I will see daylight again.

These are last word that you will never hear from me again.

It is very short time that I will be taken by the evil ghost and be dragged to another dimension of time.

I feel they are coming for me and I cannot run and I still and I feel a touch of evil behind me, now . . . .

Silent, the door shut tight and the house is dark and Josh is gone.

Low humming and humming continues . . .

Next morning the police arrive and found no bodies in the house.

The police had an investigated but no answered about Josh, and Star and Lee and Connie and the paranormal investigate missing persons and never been found and seen since unknown location since 2008.

Even today they are searching for them and no trace of them.

Author Jean Marie Rusin